PENGUIN METRO READS
LOVE KNOWS NO LOC

Arpit Vageria is the bestselling author of *You Are My Reason to Smile*, *Be My Perfect Ending* and *I Still Think about You*. He was featured in a Tata Motors documentary to inspire youngsters to read stories. Vageria also writes scripts for TV shows and award functions, such as *India's Best Dramebaaz*, *Sabse Bada Kalakar*, *Indian Idol* and IIFA Awards.

You can contact him at:
Email: arpitvageria401@gmail.com
Facebook: https://www.facebook.com/arpitvageria27/
Instagram: arpitvageria
Twitter: arpitvageria27
Phone number: +91-8451829595

ARPIT VAGERIA

Penguin
metro reads

An imprint of Penguin Random House

PENGUIN METRO READS

USA | Canada | UK | Ireland | Australia
New Zealand | India | South Africa | China | Singapore

Penguin Metro Reads is part of the Penguin Random House group of companies
whose addresses can be found at global.penguinrandomhouse.com

Published by Penguin Random House India Pvt. Ltd
4th Floor, Capital Tower 1, MG Road,
Gurugram 122 002, Haryana, India

Penguin
Random House
India

First published in Penguin Metro Reads by Penguin Random House India 2019

10 9 8 7 6 5 4 3 2

ISBN 99780143445999

Typeset in Sabon by Manipal Digital Systems, Manipal

Printed at Repro India Limited

www.penguin.co.in

MIX
Paper from
responsible sources
FSC® C047271

This is a legitimate digitally printed version of the book and therefore might not
have certain extra finishing on the cover.

CHAPTER 1

April '17

Some love stories seem to have been written in the stars; they seem to have received the benediction of some higher forces. However, make no mistake. Just like the moon might appear to be a flawless orb of white light from far away, but when peered through the powerful lens of a telescope, one finds that its face is rather pockmarked. So it is with these seemingly perfect love stories. Their timeline is marred by numerous episodes of hatred too. And what accounts for these dents? Do we really need to be incited or a trigger to hate someone? Could it maybe because we just love to hate, because hatred is ingrained in us as love is, and we simply act on our impulses? Is it simply a rule that we follow? Like India and Pakistan?

As Kabeer settled into his seat on the flight, memories of his last meeting with Zoya came flooding back. This was the last leg of his tour. It was also his last chance to restore the selectors' faith in him and secure a place for himself in India's international cricket team. On his way from the airport to the hotel in the bus with his other teammates, he read his last WhatsApp chat with her over and over again until the bus drew up at the Taj hotel in Mumbai. Even though he wanted to stay completely focused on the game to avoid disappointing his city, as he had done the last time, his thoughts repeatedly drifted to Zoya. He wondered where she was. Whether she had fallen in love with somebody else or, worse, forgotten Kabeer like a bad past and moved on.

There's enough time to watch an entire movie when commuting through Mumbai's gridlocked traffic, he thought. He wasn't aware how long he had been listening to the playlist being fed into his earphones; it had already been repeated twice or thrice; all were tracks sung by Zoya. He remembered her telling him that every song she sang was inspired by him and that she had conceptualized these lyrics in his very presence. That made him feel special.

Kabeer barely noticed the crowd of fans waiting outside the hotel, holding up placards with his name on it. The girls in the crowd frantically waved to catch his attention; some of them were wearing masks with his face painted on them—all for one smile in return.

A hand on his shoulder shook him out of his reverie. Arko was a teammate from Team India A, playing for Mumbai Riders in the T20 tournaments. He nodded to Kabeer indicating that it was time to disembark. Kabeer felt a tightness in his throat. He quickly looked around, hoping no one had noticed his emotional state.

Arko stared at Kabeer as he saw him sniffling and wiping his nose. 'This is affecting your game, Kabeer; however, I've seen you in worse phases before. You can snap out of this as well.'

'I'm just not used to being without Zoya,' Kabeer said gruffly, picking up his rucksack and moving down the aisle of the bus.

'You just have to get used to living without people who don't belong with you in the first place,' whispered Arko over his shoulder.

'She was mine.'

'She is a Pakistani,' Arko stated flatly.

'So?'

'She was a habit; you'll get over her. After what she did to you, you didn't have any other choice. There were a million things that you could have done, but you did the right thing.'

Kabeer took a moment to register his words.

'Don't blame yourself, Kabeer,' Arko encouraged. 'It wasn't your fault.'

Kabeer smiled. At times, when one has nothing to say, one falls back on meaningless gestures, such as forced smiles, handshakes, or even emoticons, hoping against hope that they would be adequate to convey one's feelings to the other person.

'Oh, you don't have to do that.'

'What?'

'Smiling forcibly. But there's one thing that you shouldn't mind doing,' Arko said and unzipped his bag, taking out a pair of sunglasses.

'If the audience finds out that a big hitter of Team India A is a crybaby, it might hurt your fan following. Go on, put these on,' he held out the shades, 'and step out like you do on the field, with a big smile. This is your comeback match.'

As they stepped out into the hazy, humid air of Mumbai, all Kabeer could see was a blur of faces, all hollering his name, desperately trying to touch him and find a way to quickly click a selfie or two. Kabeer kept pace with his team as they made their way to the hotel lobby.

The players were received with fanfare as a dozen dhols were beaten in their honour. The paparazzi quickly surrounded Kabeer, with a fusillade of questions. He thought he espied a familiar face in the crowd, an unpleasant someone from his past. He was perturbed as a feeling of gloom descended on him. Arko's shades were a perfect foil for the turbulence of his emotions and he found himself slipping back into thoughts of Zoya.

'Kabeer, are you still in touch with Zoya?' asked a journalist, shoving a mic into his face. Kabeer ignored the question and continued walking.

'Kabeer, are you still in a relationship with that Pakistani?' the same man rephrased the question. Fury surged through Kabeer, but he clamped down on it.

'Kabeer, are you still in touch with that terrorist?'

That was it. Kabeer lost his rag and leapt at the man in a blind rage. Three security guards rushed in to intercede. In the ensuing chaos, Kabeer punched the journalist, while all around them numerous cameras clicked and whirred to record the spectacle.

The press got its scoop for the day; this incident would go viral and become fodder for weeks to come.

His teammates looked embarrassed and disappointed. The coach was understandably livid, while the fans looked confused and appalled.

In a matter of sixty seconds, they went from cheering to booing him. Two minutes later, the world would know that Kabeer had lost his temper again. Three minutes later, the cricket board would expel him from the next match. And five minutes later, he would discover that the sloppy housekeeping service had missed emptying out one of the drawers in his room, thereby accidentally leaving a ray of hope for him in it.

Although it was night-time, the sky had taken on a tint of silver for Kabeer as he leaned on that faint optimism. From the balcony of his sea-view room, he gazed at the crowd beneath gradually dispersing and wondered if his fans would ever forgive him or maybe even go as far as to empathize with him.

But there's only so much one can expect from people. Nobody can restore lost loved ones or help undo one's mistakes.

The only way forward is to strive for it ourselves.

CHAPTER 2

May '16

On a Friday evening, Kabeer found himself on a bus along with some of the top players of the country. As he looked around, he realized that he had shared the field with most of these players at one point or another, but this was the first time he was going to play with them as a team at an international level. He sat back, relaxed and did a mental recap of the extraordinary turn of events that had bagged him this golden opportunity.

Two days ago, the BCCI had called to offer Kabeer a chance to play in place of Rishabh Pandey, who had suffered an unfortunate injury. Pandey was one of the best all-rounders in the team. Kabeer was determined to give his best today and not let his teammates down. Gunfire could be heard at a distance, but Kabeer remained unmoved. He was aware that these were—unlike the ones seven years ago—celebratory gunshots in anticipation of this friendly match in Lahore between India and Pakistan. He recalled the Lahore terror attack of 2009 when a bus full of Sri Lankan cricketers, along with several Pakistani policemen and civilians, was ambushed and many of those on board were injured, maimed and, some, even killed.

Considering his loathing for the country, its principles and politics, it was ironic that Kabeer's international debut was in Pakistan. As he gazed out at the passing scenery through the bus window, he saw countless people going about their daily routines. Although he couldn't hear them through the double-glazed windows and the roar of their large bus, he knew that they were speaking with each other in a language that he could easily comprehend.

Expecting to feel alien in an unfamiliar environment, Kabeer was startled by his strange empathy towards this foreign land and taken aback by its uncanny similarity to his homeland—the same shops, the same roads generously freckled with potholes, gigantic posters of political leaders and traffic rules that were flagrantly violated.

What would have happened had the Partition never taken place? Kabeer wondered. He imagined reading 'Lahore, India' on the billboards in such a world.

His thoughts were suddenly interrupted by a huge hoarding on the side of the road—a strikingly beautiful woman was featured on it, wearing a sleeveless, black sequined top and holding a mic in her hand. Her lips looked as luscious and tempting as jelly on vanilla ice cream. Kabeer was awestruck. This wonderful, marvellous being took complete control of his senses. The caption on the hoarding said she was Zoya Malik—famous Pakistani singer, with a massive fan following.

As the bus drove on through the streets, several billboards featuring her kept coming into view. She looked lovelier in each of them, and like a child seeing snow for the first time, Kabeer was wholly enchanted by her inexplicable splendour. It wasn't as if Kabeer hadn't been exceptionally attracted to a woman before, but this felt different—different how, he could not fathom. Her glowing skin seemed translucent and her midnight tresses flowed in thick luxuriant waves over her shoulders. She was drop-dead gorgeous! He felt particularly drawn to her eyes, which were deep, dark and mysterious, and pulling him in like a magnetic field.

He was entrapped in that intense and piercing gaze when the bus suddenly hit a speed breaker. This broke the spell and Kabeer looked at Arko, who was nodding off beside him.

Arko was an opener from Bengal, famous for his summary responses to fast bowlers. He revered Sourav Ganguly like a God; and one of his most well-talked-about eccentricities was his never-ending recitation of the 'Ganguly Chalisa'. Although he had met him only once, he informed every person whom he met about it and every time with a new twist—like a director taking shots from every possible angle to get the best result.

The commentary of an ongoing tennis match was crackling over Arko's earphones, but his eyes were shut. As Kabeer began to turn away, Arko took a sip from his water bottle. Surprised, Kabeer realized that he must not have been sleeping after all, unless such a condition as sleep-drinking existed. Kabeer began to look away, but it was too late. Arko suddenly opened his eyes and frowned, 'What?'

'Nothing,' Kabeer replied.

'Are you attracted to me?'

This question left Kabeer as surprised as Arko was when he had found Kabeer staring at him.

'Then why are you looking at me like that?' Arko scowled, 'is there anything I can do to help? As long as you don't want me to sleep with you.'

'It's nothing. I thought you were watching the tennis match,' Kabeer scowled back, 'and I just found it odd that your eyes were shut.'

'Oh, that! Can I tell you a secret?'

'If that doesn't make you think that I am not straight, then, yes, definitely,' Kabeer replied, although he couldn't help smiling.

Arko gave Kabeer one of his earphones. 'Now close your eyes and just concentrate on the voice of the female player. Enjoy yourself.' He increased the volume and in an instant, Kabeer understood what he had meant. The grunts the female tennis player made while playing each energetic shot sounded orgasmic.

Kabeer opened his eyes in amazement and started laughing hysterically.

'And this is your big discovery?'

'Yes, when I got bored of studying in an all-boys' school,' Arko said, with a naughty twinkle in his eyes, and Kabeer burst out laughing once again. There was something about Arko's straightforward intelligence and unforced humour that made Kabeer feel that they could be good friends.

'Do you want some more action?' Arko offered.

'Not right now, thanks, but I would certainly like to catch up with you once we start our practices in the nets,' Kabeer said. Arko replied with a brief thumbs up, before getting busy with his tennis match again.

Kabeer extracted the water bottle in the side pocket of his seat and gulped it all down in one go. Another one of those hoardings flashed past his window. It mentioned that Zoya Malik would perform at Hotel Hilton Suites, Lahore, very soon.

A sudden hatred for the British government surged through him for partitioning the country. How easy it would have been to meet her if they had belonged to the same country. No matter how unlikely it seemed, his intuition told him that they would cross paths someday.

But all his grudges against Pakistan, the Partition and the British Raj soon dissolved into nothingness as he closed his eyes and drifted off to sleep.

CHAPTER 3

April '17

Zoya ruled Kabeer's thoughts through the days that followed his tumultuous arrival in the city. He agonized, as he blamed himself over and over again, yearning to somehow undo the violent history of the two nations.

The news of his scuffle with the reporter spread like wildfire and Kabeer was suddenly daubed with the dubious distinction of being the prime target of the Indian media. A public outcry was raised against his treachery for dating a Pakistani. Some senior cricket experts even took to a newsroom debate, advising him to stay grounded and not let fame and success go to his head. Despite the prevailing chaos around him, Kabeer felt calm and at peace.

The bell rang. Kabeer did not open the door, deciding it would be best if he simply ignored everyone for a while.

'It's me! Open the door, dammit!' Arko bellowed. Much as Kabeer liked Arko, he sometimes tended to be tiresome enough to give him a headache. Arko never seemed to respect anybody's privacy, not even his own, and would sometimes take a dump with the bathroom door ajar.

As Kabeer opened the door, he shook his head at Arko and said, 'I don't want to talk about it.'

Kabeer expected Arko to persist, but instead, he merely shrugged and went over to the large leather sofa and lay down on it. Arms behind his head, he crossed his feet, as if waiting for Kabeer to speak.

'By the way, in case you're freaking out because of what happened a while ago, I should probably let you know that I am not ashamed of what I did,' Kabeer remarked coldly. He tried switching off the television, but Arko snatched the remote from him.

'Then why run away? Face those media cannibals. They're going to target everyone who is even remotely connected to you. You cannot let your close ones pay the price,' Arko said before turning up the volume.

'We tried contacting Kabeer's family to find out whether he is dealing with some medical issues post his break-up with Zoya, but his family refused to respond. His father slammed the phone down on us. Like father, like son,' said a journalist who seemed to be reporting from outside their hotel.

'It's a shame how a person who has been loved so much by the media strikes out at a journalist so viciously. Shame on Kabeer! Shame on cricket!' another news anchor shouted.

Kabeer exhaled sharply. 'You expect me to take all this seriously?'

'No, I expect you to take your career seriously. You can't keep goofing up and expect the media to turn a blind eye.'

'Where did I go wrong? Defending my girlfriend who is from another country or attacking someone who has been hounding us forever?' Kabeer snapped.

Arko sighed and looked out of the window. He could see the 'victim' reporter at a distance being interviewed by other reporters. Arko could see the winning smile on his face—the person who no one knew about a few minutes ago had suddenly become the centre of everyone's attention.

'You were wrong in defending yourself when everyone was busy attacking you, and you were wrong in attacking the reporter when he lured you into it.

'Kabeer, the best thing you could have done in this situation was not to get provoked. That was exactly what he wanted. He will receive his share of sympathy for the next few days and smirk like the devil whenever you get labelled as the villain!'

Kabeer fell silent.

'What are you going to do next?'

Kabeer extracted an envelope from his pocket and tossed it on the low table in front of the couch. Arko wordlessly took out two printouts of Zoya Malik's flight tickets. One, from Dubai to Mumbai, and another, from Mumbai to Bangalore. Both dated 17 April 2017, which was the day before.

'Is she in India?' Arko asked in amazement.

'If these tickets are to be believed, yes.'

Many had suggested that Kabeer should leave Zoya if he wanted to gain the confidence of his nation. It was true that he had been withdrawn and quiet in the last few months and had often wondered if he loved her any less. But, the answer to it was a clear and definite no.

Arko looked at Kabeer, a worried frown on his face. He remembered the first time he had talked to him about her and cried for her.

Arko always tried playing it cool, but he knew that Kabeer loved Zoya. And this time, no matter what the consequences might be, he would not be able to stop him. He mulled over it and as though reading Kabeer's mind, asked, 'You think you would be able to find her?'

'I would like to believe that there's hope.'

'And what if she says there's no way you're getting back together?'

'That would give me the much-needed closure,' Kabeer stopped pacing and sat down on the bed. Arko watched him worriedly. Kabeer smiled at him and said, 'Let's leave some questions for the journalists, my friend.'

'How will you find her?'

'At the risk of sounding soppy, I suppose I will just follow my heart, my instincts.' Kabeer grinned, '... and considering she's a celebrity in her own right, it should be easy to find events where she will be performing at in Bangalore,' he added with a wink.

'Sounds like a plan,' Arko said sarcastically.

'I wish I had other options.'

'How about the option of proving that you're serious about cricket?'

'I don't want to regret not having at least tried to get Zoya back. I need to give it one last shot.'

'That's what you said the last time.'

Kabeer chuckled, 'If there's one thing cricket has taught me, it's to *never quit*.'

'There's no point arguing with you.'

As the conversation went on, Arko found himself surrendering to his usual frustration at Kabeer's stubbornness. He was randomly packing his things into a duffel bag by now. Kabeer smiled at him in a way that bared all his intentions.

'All right, I'll talk to the coach; now get some sleep, okay? '

'Not until I find Zoya.' Kabeer felt a tightness in his throat as he moved towards the door.

He slipped out of the hotel, avoiding the lobby and boarded a cab. It was past midnight and raining heavily. There were not many cars on the road and it looked quite unlike Mumbai. Frightening thoughts kept racing through his mind, urging him to get out of Mumbai before anyone saw him.

There was a loud thud and Kabeer felt the car judder with the impact. A mob materialized out of nowhere and surrounded the car, banging their fists on the windowpanes. Kabeer and the driver froze in terror as the angry crowd mercilessly battered the car on the windows and the windshield, shouting in anger. In a few minutes, the panes of glass would shatter and furious arms would reach inside the car. Something was wrong, terribly wrong and then . . . BOOM!

CHAPTER 4

May '16

It was the day before the net practices began for the one-day match, which was scheduled for two days later. Kabeer was up early and decided to spend the next few hours walking around Lahore. He roamed around and purchased shoes for himself and sandals for his mother from Anarkali Bazaar. The market was already bustling with activity as the hawkers with their little stalls had set up shop and got ready for the day's business. He smiled to himself. These sights reminded him of the bazaars on Fashion Street or Colaba Causeway in Mumbai. Early-bird shoppers were already busy haggling. Shopkeepers sang out their offers of aromatic tea, coffee and juices, loudly grumbling when people walked past without tasting their wares.

One hawker was setting up a makeshift stall, selling T-shirts of cricketing legends. Kabeer was surprised to see that Tendulkar T-shirts seemed to be just as popular as those of Shahid Afridi.

'Don't you have Tendulkar in Pakistani uniform?' a little boy asked.

'If that were possible, we would have had more world cups than India,' the shopkeeper said gaily. Everyone around laughed.

'Do you also want Tendulkar in Pakistani uniform?' he asked Kabeer.

'No, I want Tendulkar in Indian uniform only.' Everybody turned to look at Kabeer.

'You don't sound like you're from here.'

Kabeer hesitated. 'No, I am from India.'

'What are you doing in Pakistan?'

'I am a cricketer. I am here to play a friendly match with the Pakistani team,' Kabeer replied.

There was pin-drop silence for a few seconds, and then the shopkeeper said, 'You are our brother, an honoured guest. Please come inside.' He drew back a curtain at the rear of the stall to reveal a cavernous room.

He clapped his hands imperiously at his young shop assistant, 'Ghulam, get a special lassi, samosa and chole bhature for our Indian brother.' His eyes glowed with joy and pride as he offered Kabeer the best seat in that room. Kabeer wondered for a moment if he was actually sitting in a country that was up in arms against his own. He felt a little uneasy and didn't let his guard down. However, with time, he started feeling more comfortable.

Kabeer had an animated conversation with the shopkeeper. And they bonded over stories, *gaalis*, girls, politics and, most importantly, cricket. He devoured the snacks as soon as they arrived and was pleased to see that they tasted as delicious as they did back in India. Other people from the crowd gradually joined in, noticeably intrigued by the presence of an Indian, a cricketer no less, and livened up the discussion by adding their own snippets, comparing Karachi to Mumbai and Lahore to Delhi.

It soon turned into a light-hearted competition and mockery of all things Indian and Pakistani. Kabeer found himself acting as a one-man-army when those around him began mocking an Indian journalist and the comical way in which he delivered news. To counter this, Kabeer started poking fun at an ex-army chief of Pakistan. No one seemed to take any offence whatsoever, as both sides laughed off the jabs, all in good humour. This was the very first time that Kabeer had actually interacted with local

Pakistanis, and he was pleasantly surprised at the ease with which he could join in the good-humoured banter.

'How come you're wandering around by yourself? Generally, the sports celebs never venture out without an armed escort.'

'I didn't inform anyone that I was going out.'

'Don't you feel scared?'

'Should I be?'

'Not when you're with your brothers here,' the shopkeeper smiled. His words touched Kabeer's heart deeply. With them, the few traces of fear that had remained also vanished, and in their place, a newfound sense of fraternity was established. Kabeer felt one with them and finally safe in his surroundings.

'My grandfather was born in Delhi actually,' Ghulam piped up. 'He fought for Independence only to end up in another country. He died ten years later and not once did he call himself a Pakistani. Partition did strange things to people,' he scoffed. Everybody fell silent as they pondered the point and Ghulam served refreshments.

'What were they even fighting for? If not a piece of their own land?' Ghulam exclaimed in distress. He seemed quite disturbed by the subject and smiled in pain, before settling himself down. 'So, the match is tomorrow, right?' he asked suddenly.

'Yes.' Kabeer replied.

Ghulam picked up a couple of T-shirts, one of Tendulkar and another of Afridi. 'Take these as a small gift from a Pakistani,' he said. He wrapped them up and put them into a paper bag. 'We'll come to watch the match tomorrow and for the first time in my life, I'll cheer for an Indian in Pakistan.'

With a heavy heart, Kabeer smiled and shook Ghulam's grubby hand formally. A T-shirt in the women's section suddenly caught his eye. It had a picture of Zoya Malik on it.

'I've seen posters of her everywhere. Who is she?' Kabeer asked.

'That's Zoya—the new singing sensation of Pakistan and granddaughter of Amaan Malik,' said Ghulam and chuckled, 'but that T-shirt won't suit you no matter how lean you are!'

Kabeer smiled as well. He thanked Ghulam and bade his new buddies goodbye. As he walked out in a daze, he realized what an emotional and cathartic experience this had been. He was still having a hard time digesting the events of the day.

Outside the market square, he hailed a cab. '*Bhaiya*, Gaddafi Stadium *chalenge*?'

'Indian?' smiled the cab driver. Kabeer smiled back and nodded. '*Bilkul chalenge*!' said the cabbie.

They drove past billboards of Bollywood movies. The radio in the cab was playing Shah Rukh Khan songs and *Filmfare*, an Indian movie magazine, was

23

tucked into the rear pocket of the front seat. Most importantly, the cabbie was just as talkative as any Indian cab driver. Kabeer couldn't help smiling to himself, as he settled back into the leather upholstery.

CHAPTER 5

April '17

The rear windshield glass finally gave way under the blows of the angry mob, spraying shards on to the rear seat. Kabeer looked on, terrified and panic-stricken. The car had come to a dead stop, as the driver didn't want to speed up and accidentally kill someone. He could hear them shouting, daring him to come outside. He knew that if he did, he wouldn't survive more than ten seconds. He saw an inexplicable rage in their eyes—a rage that could compel them to murder mercilessly.

Kabeer frantically looked around for anything that he could use to save themselves, but found nothing. Suddenly, somebody emptied a can of petrol on the back of the car. Kabeer felt paralysed. The driver was crying. Kabeer could hear his own heartbeats loud and clear. He watched the driver kissing his family picture for what probably was his last time. Suddenly, Kabeer leaned forward and told the driver, 'Just run when I open the door.'

The driver stared blankly at him and then gave a slight nod. Kabeer quickly opened the offside door. The cabbie slid out into the pouring rain and was immediately swallowed by the mob. Kabeer hoped he had made it out safe. A million thoughts rushed through his head. He thought about his mother who might not get to see him again; Zoya—who would probably hear of the incident on the news—would never know that he was on his way to meet her; his friends; his team; his fans. He closed his eyes and braced himself. It was a do-or-die situation. Well, maybe he could *still* die, but he was trying to keep that thought out of his mind. Taking a deep breath, he opened the rear door and quickly stepped out, and was immediately drenched in the downpour. He thought he would make a run for it, as fast as he could, when—

BANG!

Someone dropped to the floor. *So much for quick planning*, Kabeer thought. He stood transfixed, shielding himself with his arms over his head. He was expecting hard blows and pain, but to his astonishment, the crowd melted away.

Kabeer lowered his arms. The police had arrived at the nick of time. They spilled out of their van into the street and summarily dealt with the violent crowd. A gun fired into the air brought them to their senses. He had never been a big suck-up to the police, but right now, he just wanted to go and hug them straight away. The police swiftly rounded up some of the goons. They handcuffed the miscreants and packed them into the police vehicles. Kabeer learnt later that they had been sponsored by an extremist political party to punish him for associating with a Pakistani.

Shaken by the incident, Kabeer stood leaning against the cab. To his surprise, he realized the driver was back in the car and crouched behind the steering wheel. He seemed equally stunned. Kabeer shut his eyes to calm himself. This was the first time he had felt so close to death; the incident scarred him.

Somebody knew about my whereabouts. The thought was frightening. *Somebody was probably spying on me.* A strange feeling of uneasiness took over him. He quickly scanned his surroundings expecting to catch sight of someone lurking sinisterly. His thoughts flew to his family. Had he inadvertently put them in danger as well?

A moment later, one of the senior policemen approached him and asked him to get into his jeep.

'Where to?' Kabeer asked.

'You're not safe here; you should come with us to the police station for some formalities and your safety,' replied the police officer.

'Why is this happening?' Kabeer asked.

'You don't have to know everything in detail, just trust us and come along. I'll explain on the way. Remember to get your things,' the cop replied.

Kabeer was about to refuse, when he realized that that would be a stupid decision. He had faced the most brutal attack of his life and was scared to death about the possibility of it happening again. So he tossed his duffel bag into the large police jeep and climbed in. As the doors closed, he finally felt safe, after what felt like ages.

'I have a flight in a few hours from now.'

'You're not going anywhere today.'

'But this is important to me.'

'Where are you going? Haven't you just been expelled from a match?' The policeman offered him a cigarette that Kabeer politely refused.

'To Bangalore.'

'Your life could be at risk.'

'Nothing is going to happen to me now.'

'Considering how confident you sound, were you aware of something happening to you tonight as well?' another cop asked before swearing obscenely at the driver when he abruptly braked hard, tyres squealing, to avoid hitting a dog that was crossing the street.

The policeman riding shotgun swore loudly, 'Keep your bloody eyes on the road! We're not here to save dogs.'

'Did you see that? This dog wouldn't have known that it was about to die had the brakes not been applied at the right time. My point is, not everyone is as lucky as this dog.'

Nobody said anything for the next few minutes. Kabeer noticed that his hands were still trembling and clenched them into fists.

'You're safe, now, Kabeer,' the police officer reassured him.

Kabeer leaned back in his seat. He could hear the loud exchanges crackling over the police wireless in the jeep, his heart thudding loudly and policemen talking to each other and into their radios. Their voices seemed to come from a distance.

One thought led to another and he slipped into imagining what his life would have been like had Zoya not been a part of it. He knew that he would have just been concentrating on his career, leading a non-controversial life. He would probably have favoured the media a bit more and would surely not be living in fear of being rejected by his dear ones and his fans for being in a relationship with a Pakistani. He felt suffocated in the closed, claustrophobic police vehicle. He realized that he was mechanically replying to the policeman's questions. Although he could sense their animosity towards Zoya, the policemen judiciously kept a lid on their prejudices.

In order to distract himself, he took out his earphones and was about to play some music when one of the cops started playing a song on his cell phone, loud enough for everyone to hear. Kabeer stared at the man in disbelief. The song was *'Teri Yaadein'*, a hit by Zoya. Soon, everyone, including the senior-most officer started humming along with song. Kabeer furrowed his eyebrows. Just a few moments ago, these men were making rude comments against her. He felt confused and furious at such duplicity, but soon Zoya's mesmerizing voice hypnotized him and, unable to stop himself, he too started singing along with her.

'You know the lyrics by heart,' one of the cops remarked sarcastically. Kabeer ignored the jibe and smiled to himself. His memories took him far away, to that time in Pakistan when Zoya had first sung *'Teri Yaadein'*. The one memory of that night that he remembered distinctly was how breathtaking Zoya had looked. He had never seen anyone as alive and beautiful as her and he probably never would.

CHAPTER 6

May '16

Weeks turned into months; and months, into years. Finally, it was time for Pakistan to host the cricket match that everyone had been waiting for. The full moon night enhanced the brilliantly lit stadium. Shades of blue and green dominated the floodlit scene. Brilliant fireworks lit up the sky and just for this occasion, there were also customized fireworks that drew the images of Indian and Pakistani flags in the sky. Bollywood and Lollywood songs blasted in the stadium. It looked like a scene right from the Wagah border, but with a friendlier atmosphere.

The decibel levels of the commentators' voices reflected the mounting excitement of the spectators, while reporters swarmed everywhere. The prime minister of Pakistan and the defence minister of India could be seen sitting together in the VVIP area displaying great camaraderie. Every time a photographer tilted the camera towards them, they pumped each other's hands with verve and gusto. This repeated for the next four or five minutes before the dignitaries decided that they had had enough and ignored the photographers, who then found a new subject of interest—a pretty girl with a Pakistani flag painted on her left cheek and an Indian flag on the right. When a reporter asked her what that was about, she beamed into the camera and declared that she had a Pakistani father and an Indian mother so it didn't matter to her who won or lost, the important thing was that they were finally playing each other again.

The crowd was driven into a delirium of ecstasy as the two teams did the rounds of the stadium in a stately procession. People seemed delighted about the new Indo–Pak friendship, despite the underlying competitive spirit. It was the two countries' passion for cricket and sportive one-upmanship that had ultimately brought them together for this friendly match.

Before the much-awaited toss, people waited with bated breath for something, or rather, someone.

A roar rippled through the crowd as a mellifluous voice greeted everybody over the audio systems. Everybody repeatedly chanted one name in unison—Zoya.

She walked on to the stage at the far end of the stadium, radiant in a shimmering gown. Her smiling face was beamed on to the giant LED screens around the stadium. People waved posters of her, others called out to her hoping she would notice, and their cheers grew deafening as Zoya waved at the cameras and raised the microphone to her lips. The stadium fell silent when she began singing and her pure dulcet tones resonated through the grounds. It almost seemed as if the crowd had gathered for a concert instead of a cricket match.

At the window of his pavilion, Kabeer stood stock-still, spellbound by her voice. Her face on the big screen drew him compellingly. He tapped his foot to the rhythm of the song and nodded his head along with its tune. Some of the senior players exchanged meaningful looks and smirked at him. Some raised their eyebrows at his reaction, but Kabeer didn't care. It was her new pop number, which had broken the Internet and hit Kabeer's heart directly. At that moment, he fantasized meeting Zoya, instantly connecting with her, exchanging numbers, having late-night conversations with her . . . *Just another celebrity crush*, he told himself.

The crowd screamed and burst into applause as Zoya's voice rose to a crescendo at the end of the recitation before fading out.

Someone from the team said, 'Let's grab the ground, guys. We're bowling first.' Kabeer seemed a bit disoriented and vigorously shook his head to snap out of his trance.

His captain, Rehaan, was giving the team a pep talk and reiterating that they had never lost a one-day match in Pakistan and weren't going to break the trend today. He spoke about upholding the pride of their nation, and winning the match for all those soldiers and civilians who had lost their lives in terrorist attacks.

Rehaan belonged to a military family and his grandfather's exploits in the battlefield during the 1971 war with Pakistan were legendary. He had also killed terrorists attempting to broach the Indian border on several occasions.

Rehaan deliberately ignored the Pakistani prime minister's outstretched hand, although the rest of the Indian team politely shook hands with him before the match began, a solecism that raised many eyebrows. Before the players ran to take their places on the immense cricket grounds, Rehaan rounded them all into a huddle and charged them with last-minute instructions. Kabeer could feel the anger emanating from him. His eyes were bloodshot and he looked possessed by a maniacal rage. He intended to put his heart and soul into the match and wanted the team to do the same. Before dismissing the huddle, in a clear, aggressive voice, he shouted, 'Bharat Mata *ki jai*!' The team repeated it thrice after him and then dispersed.

The Indian players were suffused with adrenaline. Kabeer glanced across to the stage to see if he could catch a glimpse of Zoya, but the stage was too far away and the cheerleaders were going into their drill as the band struck up. However, a camera projected Zoya on to the big screen as she waved and smiled at the spectators. Rehaan seemed wholly unaware that the applause was for Zoya and not the Indian team.

He glowed with pride, 'If we're getting such support in Pakistan, imagine the kind of support we'll get from our crowds when we play them in India.' Arko and Kabeer exchanged meaningful looks and sniggered.

Pepsi, the soft drink company, being the sponsor of the match, boomed its jingle over the amplifiers: '10 . . . 9 . . . 8 . . . 7 . . . 6 . . . 5 . . . 4 . . . 3 . . . Oh . . . Yes . . . *Abhi* . . . !'

The twenty-over match started off very well for the Indian team and their captain was delighted. Pakistan made 178 runs and lost seven wickets and their Indian counterparts exhibited their skill, strength and talent as they chased the required total. With 3.2 overs remaining, they won the match with seven wickets in hand. Despite supposedly being a 'friendly match', the antagonism between the teams was barely disguised as sports rivalry on the field. It was evident in the cold glances and fake smiles as they shook hands.

Although Pakistan lost the match, the spectators gave a standing ovation to both the teams for a brilliant performance. Kabeer, who performed as an all-rounder in his debut, grabbed the Man of the Match award. Zoya, looking ethereal and even more beautiful than in her posters, if that were possible, gracefully handed him the trophy with a smile and husky congratulations. Kabeer smiled back at her nervously. His head buzzed every time he looked at her. He wasn't sure if he had made any impression at all on her, as she seemed to be looking anywhere but at him.

Zoya looked divine in her black dress and kohl-lined eyes. Her lips were truly as luscious as they looked on her posters. He watched her until the ceremony concluded and she disappeared into the wings. Once again he had the strange premonition that this wasn't going to be their last meeting. He desperately hoped that this feeling was mutual.

After all the formalities were completed, the exhausted teams retired to their rooms. However, Kabeer remained in the enclosure just outside the dugout, hoping to catch a glimpse of Zoya one last time and pretended to be busy with his cell phone. All of a sudden, Zoya was there, standing a mere two hundred metres from him. This was it. His only chance. He hesitated for a moment, stood up, before sitting again. Then strengthening his resolve, he took a deep breath, placed his huge silver cup on the bench and walked towards her. A bundle of nerves, but with a smile on his face, Kabeer was determined to talk to her this time.

He was almost by her side, when there were three ear-splitting blasts, one after the other. A volley of gunfire followed immediately and Kabeer dropped to the ground in panic and fear. The stadium's arena turned into a teeming mayhem as a frenzied crowd stampeded in terror. Guards hurried towards Zoya and hustled her off to safety. A helicopter materialized out of nowhere, the rhythmic beat of its blades adding to the maelstrom, as the VVIPs' Z-level security protocols swung into action.

Security personnel came for Kabeer as well and grabbed his arms. The sporadic gunshots were getting closer and more frequent. As the guards bore him away, Kabeer heard a blood-curdling scream from behind them. He twisted around, his heart coiled in terror. The security men half-carried, half-dragged Kabeer away, as he froze looking at Ghulam lying there. The poor lad's clothes were blood-soaked and tucked tightly in his arms were Indian and Pakistani flags.

CHAPTER 7

May '16

Kabeer felt badly shaken.

He had met Ghulam only two days ago and he had seemed so full of life then, intent on cheering for the Indian team. Kabeer had broken away from the guards long enough to see the defence forces carrying Ghulam away on a gurney. He was bleeding profusely, but thankfully, still breathing.

And then he heard a woman's scream. Something about the voice made Kabeer's hair stand on its end. Zoya! Without a moment's hesitation, he ran towards her. The security men collared him and dragged him, squirming and struggling, to the pre-designated safe zone.

He found the rest of his teammates and the Pakistani cricketers huddled together at the far end of the room.

He was safe now, in a huge room, which turned out to be an auditorium where there were already many other people, all anxious with worry. There were people weeping for their lost ones and bawling children who had been separated from their parents. Some of them were trying to calm each other, others seemed to have retreated into a shell-shocked silence. Everybody looked petrified, hoping for the debacle to get over soon. It was a dismal sight to behold.

There was tight security outside the room, all tense, and the soldiers were reviewing the situation with their leader in low tones. The security force that was in the room kept busy, handing out water bottles to the civilians, administering first aid where needed and taking care of the children.

Kabeer was deeply concerned about Zoya and Ghulam—the only two people in Pakistan with whom he had felt some connection. He suddenly felt very homesick and desperately alone in an alien country, away from his family, in the middle of a terrorist attack, with strangers all around.

He deeply regretted having taken his family for granted; for ignoring his mother's calls just because he wasn't be in a mood to talk; for not telling his father how much he loved him every time he considered dialling his number but didn't. He would have traded anything just to be back home, safe, surrounded by his loving family.

He noticed that there were two Indian soldiers in the room along with four Pakistani ones. A sudden volley of gunshots broke their thoughts and conversations, bringing on a hushed silence. Clearly, there were terrorists still on the loose and they had seemed closer and louder this time. When he saw an Indian soldier kissing his wedding ring, Kabeer grew hysterical. He felt certain that they would all die. Another soldier quietly crept up behind Kabeer, and clamped his strong hands on his mouth. As Kabeer was losing consciousness, he saw sinister shadows outside the window . . . the terrorists were here!

A hail of bullets rained into the room and blood spurted everywhere. The gunmen burst through the door and were welcomed with an answering volley from all sides inside the auditorium. Kabeer realized that the soldiers had corralled the cricketers at the safest possible end of the room.

'Bharat Mata *ki jai*!' he heard an Indian soldier yell before charging at the terrorists alongside a Pakistani soldier.

The fusillade of firing in the enclosed room was deafening and the silence that followed felt somehow worse. But when the dust settled, to everybody's relief, the terrorists were overpowered and the soldiers stood there, looking alert, their guns still smoking in their hands.

After a pause, one of the Pakistani soldiers peered out to ensure that the coast was clear. Everybody heaved a sigh of relief when he returned, looking confident. On some tacit understanding (perhaps it was some kind of secret army signal), the other soldiers followed him out.

One Indian soldier, however, smiled at Kabeer and hugged him to make him feel comfortable.

'Are you okay?' the soldier asked.

Kabeer thought for a moment. 'I am not sure but I trust you. Can you be with me for a while?' The soldier nodded reassuringly. Was he acting strange? Yes. But who wouldn't, in a such situation.

Kabeer felt numb as he watched people being borne away—some still alive, writhing and groaning, some deceased.

A policeman hurried over to Kabeer, 'He says he wants to talk to you. His name is Ghulam.'

Ghulam was struggling to speak. 'My friend,' he gasped, 'please don't let this incident colour your view of this country. Never let these bastards ruin the friendship of the two nations. It's—'

He broke off at this juncture, choking and coughing. The ambulances arrived with the emergency medical teams, their sirens wailing. Ghulam was rushed away on his gurney.

'Is it a matter of his life and death?' Kabeer asked a soldier who was standing nearby.

'No. It is a matter of two nations and our brothers are paying for a political ideology. That's what this is.

You people come to Pakistan and we pay the fuckin' price. That has always been the case.'

'We came here for peace,' replied Kabeer.

'. . . and it has turned into a complete disaster,' retorted the soldier.

'I'm truly sorry about that,' Kabeer felt strangely guilt-ridden.

'You should have thought about it before coming here,' the bitter soldier turned away and left. Kabeer was left standing there, dumbfounded. But he didn't want to cause so many deaths. This was supposed to have been a friendly match, a day for celebrating peace. No one should've got hurt.

With conflicting thoughts running through his mind, Kabeer made his way back to the pavilion, his head bent. He hoped that it was all just a practical joke, not particularly funny, and that someone would come running and say, 'Relax, everyone is safe.' A bundle of rags on the ground caught his eye. He squinted, trying to discern what it was. He could vaguely make out the colours in the dark— it appeared to be dark green with some white and red patches. And then it hit him. The flags of India and Pakistan were lying in a heap on the ground, intertwined, stained with blood—a subtle irony of the situation. While Pakistan was struggling with the turmoil, the world had a different story to tell.

The news of the terrorist attack had gone viral: 'A nation of terrorism hurts itself this time,' an American TV channel said. 'Terrorism may not have a religion but it sure has a nation.' An Indian channel's tickers flashed: 'Terrorism strikes Pakistan again. Not the spirit expected at sports. All sportspersons safe.'

The sound of gunfire and the terrified screams of the people at the stadium would haunt Kabeer in the years to come.

CHAPTER 8

April '17

Kabeer glanced curiously around the police station. An inebriated man was having a heated discussion with a police officer. The cop swiftly dealt three hard slaps to the man's face.

Kabeer was still drenched from the downpour and his hands trembled uncontrollably. The inspector who had accompanied him in the police vehicle asked him to pull up a chair and sit down. He sat nervously. This was the first time he was visiting a police station and it took him some time to focus. The name tag on the inspector's shirt said 'Ashutosh Pandey'. He extracted another cigarette from the inner recesses of his uniform and lit it. He leaned forward and said, 'I like the way you play. You should be opening for the team in the batting line-up.'

'I have been, since last year,' Kabeer replied. He found a handkerchief in his trouser pocket and wiped his face, which wasn't very useful because the handkerchief was also sodden. 'Oh! You were busy making waves in the gossip columns, your cricketing exploits weren't quite so much in the limelight,' Pandey laughed.

Kabeer bristled. 'Why on earth am I here? I didn't hurt anybody.'

'You were nearly killed and according to the law, it's our duty to protect you,' Pandey replied.

The drunkard kicked up a ruckus again. This time, Pandey went over and slapped him so hard that he fainted. He returned to his seat like it was mere routine to knock someone senseless. 'You're being targeted for being in a relationship with a Pakistani,' he said matter-of-factly, 'there are thousands of patriots eager to kill you at the drop of a hat.'

'So, are these "patriots" actually terrorists inciting the mobs?' Kabeer asked.

'Sure . . . you could say there are people who hire other people to do their dirty work while they themselves remain anonymous,' Pandey said. He snapped his fingers and ordered tea and biscuits.

'How do you know that?' Kabeer asked suspiciously.

'Well, you just have to trust me,' Pandey said, as Kabeer sipped his tea. It burnt his tongue, so he quickly reached for the glass of water. Pandey leaned in, lowered his voice and said, 'Or you could burn yourself like the way you just did.'

Kabeer remained quiet. He had a feeling that everybody in the precinct was staring at him. The constable who had served them tea also brought a towel for Kabeer and put it on the desk in front of him.

'Why were you going to Bangalore anyway?' Pandey asked.

'To meet Zoya.'

'You don't really care about that Pakistani any more, do you?'

'Sir, if you don't mind, that's personal,' Kabeer snapped. A junior policeman looked enraged.

'It's because of "sir" that you are alive. You have no right to be so disrespectful of him!' the junior inspector grabbed the opportunity to butter up his senior.

'Okay, so you want to meet her.'

'Yes.'

'Does she know you're on your way to see her?'

'No,' Kabeer shook his head. 'I don't even know where she is. I'll have to find out where she is in Bangalore.'

'It wouldn't be safe for you to go looking for her. You are aware now that there are violent people baying for your blood.'

'I'll do my best to keep a low profile.'

'When do you expect to come back to Mumbai?'

'I am not really sure,' Kabeer replied.

Pandey scowled at Kabeer's apparent flippant attitude, 'Get back here asap and don't do anything as idiotic as dying for love.'

Kabeer, reasonably dry by the end of this strange conversation, returned the soggy towel to the constable and collected his duffel bag. Pandey arranged for a police jeep to drop him off at the airport.

While sitting in the jeep, Kabeer thought about the people who had attacked him and the inspector who had let him go, and how fearful he had been all night.

His father, who had wanted to instil courage in Kabeer as a child, had once said, 'Never fear, come what may.' He had always encouraged Kabeer to never to give up. This was when he had taught Kabeer to ride a bicycle. His father had toughened him up to face a tough world.

Kabeer wondered whether it was wise to go looking for Zoya. What if he were attacked again and no one was around to save him? She may have moved on and could be in another relationship. His only hope was that one's past is never truly left behind.

We think of the past as a dead flower. A cold wind blowing in the midst of a nasty summer.

Kabeer kept mulling over the what-ifs for a long time and soothed himself by thanking God that he was alive. What had not killed him had only made him stronger.

CHAPTER 9

May '16

Certain ailments cannot be treated in a hospital. Those with a philosophical bent of mind attribute their suffering to destiny and karma and try to move on. Then there are others who don't even begin to heal because they remain in dread of more pain that they think is yet to be endured.

Her memories of that day were hazy. She knew she had panicked when the gunshots went off. If only she had run faster, she might have escaped unhurt. She didn't know when the stray bullet hit her arm but vaguely remembered blood spewing everywhere and being taken away in an ambulance; and then she lost track of time. Doctors in masks rallied around, doing their best to staunch the bleeding. Zoya had the rarest blood group: AB negative. Her mother had always worried about her injuring herself at school or on the playground and being unable to find suitable plasma if a transfusion was required.

She woke up to see a doctor enter the ward along with her grandfather. The doctor immediately checked her pulse, while her grandfather squeezed her hand reassuringly.

'You seem to have recovered very well,' said the doctor and a surge of relief washed over her. Although she could feel a twinge in her arm, she nodded when the doctor asked if she was feeling all right.

She could sense the tension in her grandfather and smiled at him weakly. His eyes were swimming with tears and with great restraint, he held them back till the doctor left them alone. He hugged her and began sobbing like a child. 'I don't want to lose you, Zoya. I can't even imagine what would have happened if the bullet had hit you,' he wept.

He then took a sip from the water bottle on the bedside table. Zoya clasped his trembling hands in hers.

'I'm sorry. I put you through all this.'

'No,' he replied, shaking his white mane of hair. 'It's my fault for pressurizing you to pursue music as a career.'

'I knew what I was getting into, Naanu,' Zoya said softly, 'so you see it's not your fault at all. Music is not just my career, it's my passion and that is something I'll never regret. I will always, always be indebted to you for pointing me in this direction.'

The old man looked far from convinced. Zoya realized that he was just as traumatized as she was herself, so his next pronouncement didn't come as a shock.

'Your India tour is due next week. Cancel that,' he said imperatively, in a voice that would brook no arguments.

'We'll discuss this later, Naanu. I'm tired now,' Zoya responded, trying to postpone the inevitable.

'You don't understand. I can't imagine not talking to you for the rest of my life. I want you to be the person I utter my last words to,' the old man's voice choked.

'Is that what you really want me to do?' Zoya asked. 'You want me to give up?' she added, trying to sit up. 'Naanu, you can't tell me to do this. You were always a fighter and that's what I admired the most about you.'

Her grandfather took a deep breath. 'It wasn't a lie but it wasn't the truth either, and I have had moments when I panicked and wasn't sure of returning home. I know the truth makes you uncomfortable but I can't let you continue the same way after what happened yesterday—'

'Naanu . . . .' she wheedled as she had done as a child. 'If something happens to me, you'll lose me, but

51

if I leave this midway, I'll lose myself! This bullet has made me stronger. It was always your dream for me to perform in India. And I am not going to let this opportunity pass, come what may! If there's something I've learned from you, it's to never back down.'

He smiled tenderly, 'You remind me of your mother. She was a fighter too. She would've been proud of you. She never lost any of her battles, except the last one with cancer . . .'

'She gave it a tough fight till the last moment.'

'Yes, and it's not about whether you win or lose. It's about giving it a tough fight.' Her grandfather stroked her hair. He paused for a few seconds before saying. 'You're right, *beta*. You're doing the same.'

The door of the ward burst open and in came Zoya's father, Danish. Three men from his political party accompanied him bearing flowers, balloons and boxes of chocolates. Danish came quickly to the bedside and cupped his daughter's face in his hands, 'I saw the news this morning and got here as soon as I could. Why didn't you call me? Are you all right, sweetie?'

Zoya stiffened in his embrace as usual. She faked a smile as best as she could. At a signal from Danish, one of his men stepped forward to place the gifts on the side table.

'I'm okay, Abbu. Stop fussing. I'm just tired and want to rest.'

Her father sighed theatrically, 'If I've told you once, I've told you a hundred times to stay away from this music business. If you had joined politics like your sister when you had the chance, you would not be here in a hospital bed today.'

'Half-sister,' Zoya muttered and looked away tiredly. 'This is the worst possible time to have this conversation, Abbu.'

Danish took out a roll of cash from his pocket and placed it in front of Zoya, who looked at the money in disgust.

Her grandfather looked furious but didn't utter a single word.

At that moment, a message alert beeped on her phone. Her grandfather handed the phone to her. Ignoring her father and his henchmen, she clicked open the message:

'Your visa application has been denied. Reason unstated.'

Her father smiled at her, 'Just take care of yourself and remember, your father is always here to help you with the ups and downs of life . . .' He walked out of the ward followed by his retinue.

CHAPTER 10

April '17

As Kabeer gazed at the moon high up in the sky, he realized how controlling it could be at times. No matter how much people loved stargazing, it was always the moon that stole the show.

It was almost 1 a.m. when the flight finally took off. The lights inside the aircraft were switched off and everybody seemed to be sleeping peacefully. Kabeer, however, was wide awake, his mind a maelstrom of churning thoughts; thoughts about the recent and not-so-recent events; thoughts of Zoya.

He was determined to ensure that his family wasn't exposed to any kind of trouble because of his foolhardiness. He knew they were worried. He shut his eyes and willed himself to sleep in order to give himself a break from an eventful, nightmare of a day. Drifting of, he remembered the day he had reached India after the terrorist attack in the Lahore stadium.

* * *

May '16

When the plane landed, the team was met by the press waiting for them right outside the airport. Cameras clicked furiously as the cricketers stepped into the foyer, reporters shouting out questions all at once.

'How did you feel during the terrorist attack?'

'Do you regret going to Pakistan?'

'Would you dare to go back again?'

The team was dog tired both by the journey and the nerve-wracking incident they had experienced in Lahore barely a few hours ago. All they wanted was to go home safe and sound.

As Kabeer moved slowly down the airport passage, he saw their fans welcoming the winning team. The crowd seemed subdued and worried for the intrepid team that had returned triumphantly and safely despite the attack on foreign soil.

Kabeer's parents were heroically holding back their tears. His grandfather was standing there holding his kid brother's hand. Kabeer hurried towards them, shouldering his way through the throng. When he reached his family, he hugged them all together in a big embrace.

'I am so happy to see you, beta,' his mother said.

'I am happy to see you too, Ma.'

'We thought we'll lose you bhaiyya, and your mobile phone was also not reachable,' Kabeer's brother piped up.

There was a huge lump in Kabeer's throat, but he smiled bravely. He turned around and waved to Arko and his coach as they left with their respective families.

As they were exiting the airport premises, Kabeer caught a news flash on the television in the foyer: 'Zoya Malik recovering fast after the attack last night.'

He wasn't sure how to react to a news like this. He was glad that Zoya had survived, but did she even care about what happened to him? Why would she? It was not as if they knew each other at all.

As they drove towards Pune, Kabeer busied himself with music, searching for Zoya's songs and playing them on a loop. For some strange reason, he felt as if listening to her songs would take him a step closer to her.

His mother, excited that her son had returned safely, was chattering non-stop about his favourite dishes. His father was also uncharacteristically talkative. He had taken a whole week off from work to spend time with his son. His brother, Karan, was an inveterate chatterbox anyway. Only his grandfather was silent during their journey home. His resentment towards Pakistan was quite apparent and nobody felt comfortable discussing the incident any more.

When they reached home, people on the street welcomed Kabeer warmly with garlands and sweets. Kabeer plastered a smile on his face. He was very tired. As soon as he entered his home, he stretched out on the large leather sofa and switched on the air conditioner. He felt glad to be back home.

Karan lay down on the diwan and switched on the television.

Kabeer groaned. 'Can't you see how tired I am?'

'Why don't you go and sleep in your room then?' Karan replied.

'Because it doesn't have air conditioning,' Kabeer snapped. 'Papa, I've told you so many times to install an air conditioner in my room, but you never listen to me.'

'I am waiting for the Diwali offer, beta. We'll get a good 20 per cent discount and a year's extended service.'

Kabeer scowled.

'If I were in charge of the finances in this house, I would have installed air conditioners in every room by now,' his mother said, coming in with fruit juice in tall glasses. She put the tray down on the teapoy, picked up the TV remote and switched from channel to channel looking for her favourite programme. Kabeer suddenly got up and snatched the remote from her hand.

He increased the volume as a news reporter said, 'Last night our cameras captured a unique and heart-warming sight in the land of terror. A young shop assistant, Ghulam, breathed his last a while ago, clutching both the Indian and Pakistani flags to his chest. Another incident during this terrible attack was . . .'

Kabeer switched off the TV at this point. His mother tentatively reached for him. He put his arm around her and haltingly told his family about his meeting with Ghulam. He couldn't even bid him goodbye. He couldn't even tell him that he didn't deserve to die like that. Kabeer felt as if he had lost a family member.

CHAPTER 11

June '16

As soon as she was discharged from the ward, Zoya promptly reapplied for an Indian visa. Her first ever show in India was scheduled to take place in a little over a month's time. The visa office invited her to attend an interview at the end of a fortnight.

The day of the visa office appointment dawned clear. Some of the people in the department, both employees and other applicants, recognized her when she arrived. They started whispering among themselves. Not knowing what to do, they offered her their sympathies. Zoya smiled and nodded at them, and then pretended to be immersed in a magazine while she waited. It was almost an hour before she was finally summoned to the inner sanctum for the interview.

The walls of the room were covered with pictures of the country's leaders. The interviewer bade her to sit down as soon as she entered the room.

He offered her a glass of water, which she graciously took a sip from as she leaned back on her seat.

'You sing very well,' he began conversationally. Zoya glanced at his name tag, 'Shafiq Ansari', and nodded in graceful acknowledgement of the compliment.

'I see that this will be your first visit to India,' he said, rapidly scanning over her application documents.

'Yes, sir,' Zoya replied succinctly. She knew that this wasn't going to be easy, given the circumstances, but she wanted to give it her best shot.

'Why do you want to go to India?' he asked.

'It's going to be my first international concert, that's why,' Zoya replied.

'A lot of people have gone to India to make their careers, but what have the Indians done? They have thrown them out heartlessly. Those who failed to make their mark in India have sat on that very same chair that you are sitting on right now. None of them heeded my advice and suffered. Nobody is willing to employ them even in Pakistan now.'

If the rest of the meeting was also going to be along these lines, Zoya felt that her chances of securing a visa was growing less likely with each passing second.

'Do the Indians pay you well?' Shafiq asked.

'They pay better than Pakistan, but it's not about the payment,' Zoya said.

'Then what is it about?'

Zoya paused for a bit, 'It's about amicable relations between the two nations.' The interviewer didn't bother to disguise his scepticism, but Zoya rallied and continued, 'I feel that performing in India could go some way to bridge the ever-widening gulf between Pakistan and India. Music is an art that unites people, regardless of nationality, and I would like my art to be an ambassador for peaceful co-existence.'

'According to your bank statement,' Shafiq scowled, extracting it from the sheaf of documentation she had submitted along with her application form, 'there's no consistency in your income.'

'As an artist, I earn on project-basis and not on monthly basis,' Zoya clarified.

'But that's a demerit when applying for a visa outside the country. There's the danger that you may extend your stay in India to earn more, or worse, you may opt to never return to Pakistan.'

'Their government will extradite me if I attempted to do that.'

'Then you might consider changing your identity. But that would be another crime.'

'I sincerely hope you're not serious, sir.'

'We live in a country that is time and again accused of being a terrorist state by India. Why would a self-respecting Pakistani stoop to perform in a foreign country that makes no secret of the fact that it considers us terrorists?'

'Not all of them do, sir. And for those who do, I am determined to refute their groundless allegation. I am sure that the cricket team that came here for a friendly match had hoped to establish good ties with our country. It is very unfortunate that they only took back unpleasant memories that will haunt them forever.'

'It looks like you're already speaking their language. Money makes the strangest of bedfellows. They say artists have a rich soul and it looks like you've already sold yours to India,' Shafiq's lips twisted into a humourless smile.

'Strange sentiments indeed from a visa officer, sir,' Zoya fumed, unable to hide her irritation. 'However,' she was not quite ready to throw in the towel as yet, 'your position deems it necessary that you abide by the visa laws and not follow your personal bias.'

'So, you are determined to fly in the face of your nation's sentiments?'

'Travelling abroad doesn't automatically boil down to treason, sir.'

The outer door suddenly slammed shut; Zoya and Shafiq realized that their conversation had been clearly audible to the people sitting outside.

'I can see that you have applied for a six-month visa,' Shafiq said brusquely after an embarrassed silence.

Zoya nodded.

'I'm willing to give you a one-month visa.'

'But my show is after thirty-two days,' Zoya protested.

'Madam, if you're sure that India wants to co-exist with us in peace, I'm fairly sure they'll be able to sort out your concert dates,' Shafiq sneered.

Zoya let it go and accepted the thirty-day visa and left the room with her head held high. As she stepped out of the building, she took a deep breath and looked around. Despite the numbered days of her visa, she felt elated at finally being granted the opportunity to visit India. She was aware that her house of cards could yet come tumbling down if the organizers refused to move the dates around. But she was determined to stay positive and optimistic.

CHAPTER 12

June '16

The event organizers in India found themselves in a quandary. They had to radically restructure Zoya Malik's schedule. It spoke volumes of their organizing skills when they soon telephoned the budding star to say that her international debut had been rescheduled and that she need not worry about any of the other arrangements either.

The only thing that didn't match Zoya's expectations was the room she was promised. However, a simple note of apology from the organizers, along with a box of her favourite chocolates, cheered her up.

The performance was to be held exactly a month after the terrorist attack in Lahore's stadium. Zoya realized that she was on very thin ice as far as international diplomatic relationships were concerned. It was like attempting to reconstruct a bridge that had been burnt down several times.

Nevertheless, Zoya was determined not to let any negativity mar the enjoyment of her sojourn in India. She was on the telephone with her grandfather, describing in detail all the wonderful things she had seen, punctuated with exclamations about the similarity between their countries. The old man closed his eyes, enraptured by the picture she painted.

'It's so nice to get so much love from across the border, Naanu. They're just like us!'

'Yes, yes, beta, just take care of yourself, though.'

'I will, Naanu. Nothing will happen to me,' Zoya assured him. 'Love you, Naanu. See you soon,' she said and hung up just as the doorbell rang. It was room service bringing her the dinner she had ordered. One whiff and she felt like she was back in Pakistan.

Replete after an eminently satisfying dinner, Zoya decided to stroll in the park outside the hotel. This was exclusively for VIPs. Mentally rehearsing her songs, she didn't really pay attention to the very few people around her, and most definitely did not notice the Indian cricketer approaching her.

Kabeer smiled hesitantly when Zoya suddenly realized he was standing there, directly in front of her. Zoya smiled back awkwardly, not knowing what else to do.

'Do we know each other?' she asked.

She was looking divine as always. Kabeer couldn't help but notice how luscious her lips were, even without any lip gloss. 'Excuse me,' Zoya frowned and repeated, 'do we know each other?'

Kabeer was hauled back to reality.

'We've met once,' Kabeer stammered. 'We were formally introduced. We were in the same stadium during the Lahore attack, nearly a month ago now, when I was a part of the Indian cricket team. You gave me the Man-of-the-Match trophy,' he smiled.

Zoya glowered at him. 'How can you even talk about that and smile?'

'Oh! no, no. I wasn't smiling because I was happy about that calamity. I was smiling because, you know, I saw you and remembered you from that day. You sing fabulously,' Kabeer replied.

Zoya smiled, 'Thanks.'

With some kind of non-verbal mutual consent, they walked back to the entry gate together. Kabeer carefully maintained the required distance between them and hoped that his heartbeats were not loud enough for Zoya to hear.

'So where were you when, you know . . . ?' Zoya trailed off.

'During the terrorist attack?'

'I didn't want to say it, but yes.'

'Why mustn't we say "terrorist attack"?'

'Because I just want to forget that day ever happened. So, where were you?'

'I was on the field when it started. In fact, I was just standing a few feet from you.'

'Oh.'

'Yes. I ran towards you when the bullet hit you, but my team's bodyguards dragged me away to the safe zone.'

'How filmy, right?' Zoya laughed. Just then her watch beeped to indicate that she had completed her quota of a thousand steps for the day.

'I never would have taken you for a fitness freak.'

'Ah. But then everyone has got to be fit—be it a singer or a sportsman.'

Kabeer chuckled, 'Yes. Definitely helps when we're running from terrorists.' Kabeer's attempt at humour did not go down well with Zoya and she frowned at him and walked away.

'Is that what you people consider us Pakistanis?'

'Why do you say that?'

'That's what I've heard.'

'I've also heard that Pakistani girls are beautiful,' Kabeer looked at Zoya apologetically.

'What do you mean?' Zoya asked. 'Even if they are, it's a condescending and patronizing thing to say . . . and insulting.'

'You're the first Pakistani girl I've ever spoken to. And if you weren't so beautiful and interesting, I wouldn't have run all the way from the fifth floor just to see you when I have a practice session at 5:30 in the morning,' he said and bit his lips.

'How did you know that I was here?' she asked suspiciously.

'From your Facebook status today.' Seeing her doubtful expression, he added, 'I swear I didn't stalk you. I'm staying in the same hotel for a few days. I came here tonight hoping to run into you. I didn't mean to alarm you,' Kabeer put up his hands in a surrendering gesture.

'It's not that. Because of the cricketers here, I had to compromise with a much smaller room than I was promised,' she said bitterly.

'You can share my room,' Kabeer said nonchalantly. But as soon as he realized what he had said, he clarified, 'I meant, you can take my room and I can sleep in yours. We can swap rooms, is what I meant.'

'You have this way of offering things to girls, is it? You put your life in danger almost taking a bullet for me and now the luxurious suite. Never realized Indians were so kind,' Zoya said, smiling.

'Sure we are,' Kabeer grinned, 'just don't ask for Kashmir.'

'I could say the same to you; we have our own Kashmir,' she retorted and they both laughed.

'It took many summits to discuss Kashmir and it took us less than a minute to resolve it,' Kabeer said.

'We haven't resolved it yet.'

'I am glad; this way we'll have more meetings to discuss this serious issue. Coffee?' Kabeer asked.

Zoya chuckled at his offer.

'The more you get to know me, the more will I surprise you,' Kabeer prophesied mysteriously.

'I like the sound of that. Coffee, then,' she agreed.

'Sure, neighbour,' Kabeer grinned and gallantly gestured to her to precede him into the in-house coffee shop.

CHAPTER 13

June '16

Despite nation-wide protests against a Pakistani artist performing in Mumbai, the event kicked off to a great start. The Andheri sports club was full of fans, agog to see and listen to Zoya. A popular Indian singer inaugurated the concert programme.

Zoya was amazed at the adulation she received. She got an adrenaline rush seeing thousands of people rooting for her, posters held high. It was like a dream come true to see the auditorium packed to the rafters with 40,000 music lovers who didn't hold her nationality against her.

She was still waiting in the wings, about to go onstage a few minutes, when her phone buzzed in her pocket. It was a call from Pakistan. She slipped into an anteroom that was comparatively quieter.

'Zoya,' said a deep voice.

'Mamu?' Zoya replied, surprised to get a call from her maternal uncle. From the tone of his voice, she knew something was wrong. The last time he had called was to tell her about her mother's unfortunate and sudden death. As always, she was taken aback at how similar he sounded to her grandfather.

'Abbu isn't well, my dear. His liver failed and he had a heart attack last night. Doctors are saying that chances are slim that he'll make it,' said Mamu worriedly.

Zoya couldn't speak for the lump in her throat. After she had finished her conversation with Mamu, she did her best to focus on the job in hand—the concert. She was grief-stricken when her name was announced, but she quickly composed herself, took a deep breath and stepped out on to the stage. The audience gave her a clamorous welcome. Her *aalap* (prelude) won the hearts of everyone present as her golden voice cast a spell solely its own.

Her sorrow under wraps, she put on her game face and sang through the evening to thunderous applause and demands for encores. She tried to imagine Naanu in the crowd, cheering for her. She imagined him running on stage to hug her when she sang his most difficult number.

In her mind's eye, all she could see was her grandfather on his deathbed. She wished she had listened to him when he had tried to prevent her from coming to India. Zoya's heart wasn't in her performance and she couldn't wait for the night to end so she could return home to her grandfather. Her eyes bright with unshed tears, she soldiered on through her concert.

The auditorium reverberated with the finale of her most recent number '*Mil Jana Phir Toh Kahin*' as it faded into a whisper. The stage lights went off and the anchor announced a ten-minute intermission.

One of the crew ran up with a glass of fruit juice and a bottle of mineral water, both of which she waved away. She prayed desperately for a miracle to restore her grandfather to good health and take her to his sickbed pronto.

She hurried to her vanity van. Kabeer, who was casually leaning against the vehicle, straightened up and said, 'Congratulations! You're getting all the accolades you deserve.'

Zoya opened the door and stared at Kabeer for a second before slamming the door in his face.

The rumour mills and gossip columns were triggered. The remorseless media labelled Zoya as a diva with an attitude, given to throwing tantrums and making life a misery for her event organizers. Others saw her in the light of a victim being unfairly targeted for being a Pakistani.

In the meantime, news of Amaan Malik's deteriorating health made headlines.

In the privacy of her vanity van, Zoya desperately tried to call Mamu. At long last, he answered her call.

'Mamu, is Naanu any better now?' Zoya waited impatiently for him to answer. She tried to find something to hold on to and finally grasped the back of her chair tightly. Her knuckles had turned white.

'He's in coma, my dear, and the doctor says that it's unlikely that he will ever regain consciousness,' Mamu carefully replied, trying to keep his words as clear as he could without twisting them.

With time running out of her hands, she stood upright, trying to compose herself, and said, 'Are you beside him now, Mamu? Can you put the phone to his ear, please, so Naanu can listen to me?'

'Sure, go on then.'

'Naanu,' she whispered, 'you may not be with us when I get home tomorrow. I so wish that you didn't have to leave us. You taught me to stay positive through all of life's ups and downs. I had only heard of superheroes in stories, Naanu, till I found one in you, and you know what superheroes do? They spend their lives protecting their people, and you have always been a superhero to me, fighting my battles. Now, I will be fighting my own battles and you won't be around to protect me any more. But you've made me strong enough to face the world and win.

'Just close your eyes, Naanu, and imagine walking with me on the beach where you taught me how to take my first steps. It was such a beautiful day when you held me in your arms. But do you know what moved me the most? It was your belief in me whenever I fell and failed in certain portions of this chapter called 'life'. You were brave and courageous. Now that you're leaving, I just want to tell you how lucky I am to have had you in my life. Rest assured that I would no longer lose any battles in life and I would be the same brave and courageous person that you are and always taught me to be. Now it's time for you to give Ammi some love. She has waited for you for a long time and it's her turn to be reunited with her father. It's my turn to bid you goodbye. That's probably the last and the most difficult thing I ever wanted to do, but here I am, saying adieu with a happy face because you said you wanted me to be the person who spoke to you last.

'Have a safe journey, Naanu, in a better world, in a better place. Goodbye. I love you.'

She disconnected the call with tears in her eyes. And thousands of miles away, her grandfather breathed his last, as if he had just been waiting for his princess to bid him goodbye.

She sank into the sofa, turned the lights off and cried her heart out as she received the message from her Mamu 'Abbu jaan is no more.'

It's never easy to see the person you love the most leave you. Sometimes, you just want it to be a bad dream and sometimes, you just wait for it to pass. But when you come out of the darkness, you find that the truth is the light that's outside and the truth is that the person you loved has already started another journey elsewhere. To a place where you wouldn't be, where they would be dear to someone else, leaving memories and a lifetime of pain behind.

Everything in the world has a fix but, sadly, emotions don't.

CHAPTER 14

June '16

Some tears never dry, no matter what. Zoya gazed at her reflection in the mirror. Her make-up was in a shambles—mascara streaming down her cheeks, foundation patchy—so she rubbed it off with the tissue she had used to wipe off her tears.

As the clock ticked nine, she washed her face, quickly reapplied her make-up and practised her smile a couple of times. She was unconvinced, but it was time to go back in the spotlight, which she did, smiling broadly, and sang her most popular English number 'Memories Never Die'.

The entire auditorium resonated with the chant 'Zoya! Zoya!' And from one corner of the auditorium, one could hear: '*Iss Duniya Ki Hum Hai Shaan*, Hindustan Pakistan!'

Only Kabeer noticed the slight break in her voice as she dedicated her next song to her grandfather, a song that was originally sung by the maestro himself.

'I'll now be performing a number originally sung by my Naanu, which is loved by all of you. Through this song, I would like to tell him how grateful I am for everything that he has done for me. Naanu, I hope you're listening to this,' Zoya said, as the orchestra struck up the lilting prelude.

There was pin-drop silence when her voice faded out at the end of the rendition. Zoya didn't wait to take her bows. She left lest her emotional barrier broke.

Kabeer was again waiting by her vanity van.

'What's wrong, Zoya? I know we haven't known each other for long, but I can sense that you're upset.'

She couldn't hold back the hot tears. Kabeer impulsively put his arms around her to offer comfort. 'My Naanu is no more,' she choked, '. . . he passed away while I was performing.'

'No matter what I say, mere platitudes cannot mitigate your pain and grief at this moment,' he said softly into her hair. 'But the best way for you to bid farewell to him was by performing his very own song in India.'

Zoya drew back a little and smiled a watery smile at the tall cricketer.

'I'm sure he was waiting to speak to me. He always wanted me to be around whenever he was ready to go to heaven.'

'Yes, he has gone to a better place now,' Kabeer smiled.

'Yes. A place of his own. I remember him saying that when he dies, he wants to go to a place where my mother lives and restart their lives once again. He always used to say that she was the best child one could've ever hoped for. He regretted that he couldn't do much about her estrangement with her husband. He always had affairs. As much as Naanu tried giving his daughter the justice she deserved, he failed.'

Kabeer offered her a bottle of water, from which she sipped gratefully and hiccupped a couple of times before bravely stemming her tears.

'I need to rush back home to Pakistan but there's no flight until tomorrow morning,' Zoya said.

'Then we'll ensure you get on a flight first thing tomorrow,' Kabeer replied.

'Thanks, Kabeer.'

'For what?'

'For giving me a shoulder to cry on. I'd like to go to the airport right away and wait there for my flight. That way I'll feel closer to Pakistan.'

Kabeer immediately made a couple of calls and while he was still on one, showed her a thumbs-up to indicate that her tickets were ready and she was good to go.

When he disconnected the call, Zoya said, 'The chauffeur they'd assigned to me was very efficient. I'm going to miss him,' she sighed. 'I've asked him to collect my luggage from the hotel and meet us at the airport.'

'Life is so strange that I'm scared to get attached to anyone,' she muttered to herself. 'I can't believe that he's gone . . .'

'You mustn't let the vacuum of loneliness suck you in, Zoya. Just think of all the happy moments you've shared, that way he will always be alive within you for as long as you live.'

'Are you prepared for your parents' death?'

Kabeer was shocked.

'That's exactly how I feel at this juncture: in shock,' Zoya said.

'I understand,' Kabeer said. He started his car, 'We'll have coffee at the airport. I can't think of anything better,' he added sheepishly.

'That would be the best thing at the moment,' Zoya replied. They chatted about inconsequential matters on their way to the airport. It helped lighten Zoya's mood. Neither Kabeer nor Zoya realized how easily they bonded and established a rapport. It all seemed so natural.

When they reached the airport, they kept a low profile, doing their utmost to stay under the radar and avoid undue attention. However, to their annoyance, Amaan Malik's sudden death had aroused the paparazzi, which had quickly traced Zoya and followed her to the airport. Both celebrities in their own rights, Kabeer and Zoya were bombarded with questions and flashing cameras even before they entered the airport lobby.

'So, miss Malik, is money is more important to you than the death of your grandfather whose legacy you've inherited?' a journalist shouted.

Both Zoya and Kabeer looked astounded, and wordlessly entered the lobby of the airport.

CHAPTER 15

June '16

The previous day's events played through her mind as she set off for home from Lahore's airport. She wondered what she had done to be at the receiving end of such hostility. Why did the media imagine that she was mercenary and avaricious? Was this the price of fame and success?

She knew she had to remain strong to face the day and fought back the tears that threatened to spill out. Her Naanu wouldn't want to see her so broken up.

A crowd had gathered around the house when she reached home. Kind friends and relatives had also come to offer their support. She hurried in, looking for her Mamu and suddenly realized that her own kith and kin were subjecting her to hostile glares. She just needed to find her Mamu before she could deal with this animosity. She ran into the inner room expecting to see him, but only saw her lamenting Mami surrounded by several other women.

'Where's Mamu?' asked Zoya, kneeling by her aunt's armchair.

'You're late, Zoya baby; he must be on his way back after your grandfather's funeral rites. He'll be here soon.'

'How could the funeral take place without me?' Zoya exclaimed in shock.

'They didn't know when you would be back and decided not to wait. The dead have to be relieved as soon as possible so they can begin their journey to heaven, beta.'

'But I specifically told Mamu to wait for me and he agreed!'

'We have to abide by the society's rules, baby, so unfortunately not everything can happen at our convenience. You visited an enemy country, against your Naanu's wishes, and see what happened.'

'How is my trip to India even relevant in this context?'

'Because if you were here, your grandfather would have been alive right now. He would have got timely treatment in the hospital,' Mami snapped. 'To be honest, you were just as careless and irresponsible at the time of your mother's death.'

Zoya's heart sank in the face of such harsh criticism. Naanu, the one person who had always championed for her, was now no more. This fact now came home forcibly. Suddenly, everything had changed. She felt like a stranger in her own house without her beloved grandfather.

She softly stole away to her wing of the house. Some of their friends and relatives were also there, sharing stories about her grandfather.

One of them said, 'Amaan Ali sahib and I used to catch up for drinks often.'

Zoya knew that her grandfather disliked alcohol. Disgusted by these lies, she knew that if she stayed any longer, she would lose her temper. She abruptly left the group and went into Naanu's room, seeking comfort and solace.

The moment she stepped in, she felt better; Naanu was watching her from a distance, telling her to smile and be strong. She almost felt his gentle hand on her head and stood very still, not wanting to let go of the moment. She sensed his voice whispering to her and then it suddenly went quiet. She opened her eyes, shaking herself out of the trance and looked around the room. This was home—even if the rest of the house didn't feel like it any more. She ran her fingers over Naanu's walking stick lovingly. She picked up his spectacles from his desk and gently wiped the lens with a soft cloth and carefully replaced them in the case. She opened the wardrobe and took out his favourite shirt and buried her face in it. The floodgates burst as his scent flooded her senses and she broke down.

Nothing would bring him back now; he was gone forever and she just had to live with it.

Her telephoned pinged with a message from Kabeer: 'Are you home safe, Zoya? I know that this is a difficult time, but remember, there's a shoulder to lean on just across the border. Call me anytime you like, I promise to do my utmost to cheer you up.'

CHAPTER 16

April '17

The airline's automated announcement interrupted Kabeer's sleep and he stirred, disoriented. A tap on the shoulder by the fellow passenger beside him woke him up fully. Even as he made his way to the luggage carousel, he could hear the thunder of Bangalore traffic.

He got into his cab as the driver asked, 'Where to?'

'The Lalit Ashok hotels,' Kabeer replied. Before they could sally forth, however, the cab driver got into a loud argument with the parking attendant who claimed that the cab had been parked at the airport for ten minutes, which was the minimum time a vehicle could stay before the parking fee kicked in, but the driver protested that he had been there for exactly nine minutes. After a loud and protracted wrangle, the cabbie finally gave in and paid the fare, grumbling all the way to the hotel.

'These south Indians always do this!' the cabbie cursed under his breath.

Kabeer, who already had too much on his mind, gazed out of the window and ignored the driver.

He was still shaken by the previous night's attack on his cab. Also, he had no idea how his meeting with Zoya tonight would pan out. Although the thought of rejection was daunting, on some level he was looking forward to seeing her again.

As much as he knew he loved Zoya, there was no telling if she still had the same feelings towards him or not.

'Sir, if you want to drink water, there's a bottle of mineral water in the seat pocket before you. Would you like to listen to some music?'

'Yes, please. Turn on the radio,' Kabeer replied quickly to curtail any further attempts at conversation.

'I've seen you play cricket, sir. You play like Virat Kohli. Very aggressive. But you've got to learn to defend as well sometimes,' the cabbie turned on the radio after this word of advice and Kabeer heaved a sigh of relief.

The news crackled over the radio: '. . . cricketer, Kabeer, was attacked in Mumbai by a violent mob near his hotel. Luckily, he survived because the police arrived in the nick of time.'

The cab driver looked stunned as he heard the news. He glanced at Kabeer through the rear-view mirror. Kabeer slumped back in his seat as he sensed another conversation commencing and couldn't help looking heavenwards, asking god to give him strength.

'Sir, never knew you had a good defence as well,' the driver said tentatively, smiling. Kabeer chose not to reply.

'Can I ask you one question, sir?' he continued.

Kabeer sighed, looking out of the window at the heavy traffic.

'How is Zoya madam?' he asked.

'That's impertinence,' replied Kabeer loftily.

'I am sorry, sir. Didn't mean to pry but I was really happy when I got to know about an Indian dating a Pakistani. *Aakhir Sania Mirza ka badla bhi to kisiko lena tha na*,' he said and started laughing. '*Hamari Sania ko wo le gaye, unki Zoya ko hum le aaye. Hisab barabar*,' he added, chuckling.

Kabeer clenched his fist and clamped down on his temper. He glared at the cab driver through the mirror. As he made a U-turn and by Toit Brewpub, Kabeer suddenly lurched forward and told him to stop the car immediately.

This was the pub where Kabeer and Zoya often partied. On the pavement outside the tavern was a tall girl in a sheathe-like black dress with her back to the street, and all Kabeer could see of her was her long dark hair. She was surrounded by a group of people.

'Sir,' the cab driver protested sensing his fare dwindling, 'your hotel is quite some distance away.'

'Never mind. Stop here, please.' The driver slowed down and stopped at the kerb. Kabeer grabbed his bag, stepped out of the cab, his eyes fixed on the girl across the street, and did a dangerous dash through the traffic. As he drew closer, the girl slowly raised her chin and looked straight into his eyes.

Hope faded away as he looked into the stranger's eyes. She had looked so much like Zoya from a distance. He stood there, his hands on his knees, trying to catch his breath and cursing himself for being an idiot.

His eyes filled with tears as a flame that had suddenly started burning within him extinguished within seconds. Pedestrians swarmed around him, loudly reprimanding the man who had caused such a disturbance in the traffic. Some of them recognized him after a few moments, realization slowly dawning on their faces. He shouldered his way through the crowd and vehicles back to his cab. People had started clicking pictures with their cell phones by then.

The cabbie opened the door for him and didn't say a single word for the remaining part of the journey. Kabeer leaned his forehead on the window glass and stared out into the distance, hardly noticing the bumper-to-bumper traffic. His thoughts were far away, about Zoya. Would he ever see her again?

Disembarking at the hotel, Kabeer shook his head, trying to clear his thoughts. He clearly remembered the day he had spent there with Zoya when they had missed their flight to Mumbai a year ago.

At the hotel reception, Kabeer specifically asked to be allocated room number 1002. The room abounded with memories of the best time of his life, time he had spent with Zoya.

When he opened the door, everything came alive before him. The couch where they had made love was still there and the view through the large French windows was still as beautiful.

'Would you like to order something from room service, sir?' asked the bellboy as he deposited Kabeer's duffel bag on the luggage rack.

'A bottle of red wine and a tray of cheese, please,' replied Kabeer foreseeing a long sleepless night before him, beset by memories and regret for what could have been.

He pulled open the top drawer of the chest of drawers to unpack his meagre belongings from his bag and nearly dropped everything he was holding in his hands. There, in the empty drawer lay another e-ticket of Zoya's next flight. He could barely believe his eyes.

When he recovered from his shock, he carefully scanned the room hoping against hope that there was more than just the one clue. He focused on the areas that he thought Zoya might have considered special, but unfortunately, he didn't find anything more. He scrutinized the boarding pass. Zoya was going to be in Delhi that day. His heart sank as he realized his trip to Bangalore had been in vain

He wondered whether it was actually another step towards finding Zoya or somebody's sadistic idea of a sick joke.

In a day full of unexpected turns of events, it was with hope that he checked out of the hotel within fifteen minutes of checking in. The next flight to Delhi could change his life forever, but he had to be very careful because if it was someone else, not Zoya, orchestrating this wild goose chase, that person was stalking him like a real professional.

CHAPTER 17

July '16

The clouds had turned steadily orange as evening approached and a brisk wind rustled through the leaves of the trees. With the weather bureau dithering about the forecast, people were undecided about whether they should opt for their two-wheelers—much better to navigate through the city's traffic congestions—or four-wheelers that could afford a modicum of shelter in case the clouds burst. But another storm raged within Zoya.

Seated in the balcony, facing Naanu jaan's favourite chair, she thought of all the happy times that they had shared, lively conversations about music—modern-day music as well as the old classics—and her grandfather's wry witticisms that invariably made her laugh. He often spoke about his yearning for peace between India and Pakistan.

Today, it was Mamu jaan sitting across from her, to stake his claim to the property of his deceased father—property that had already been bequeathed to his granddaughter, Zoya.

The possibility of losing everything to her powerful Mamu jaan left Zoya with a fear of not being able to stop the injustice that would happen to her dead grandfather's wishes. 'What would you like to have, tea or coffee?' Zoya asked, disguising her anger.

'Nothing.'

'You sure about that? You always liked tea.'

'Yes. I don't like it any more,' he said and yawned, 'let's not pretend that we have ever shared a good relationship, Zoya, and get down to brass tacks.'

Zoya sipped her cup of green tea, 'Go on, then, Mamu. What is it you wanted to talk to me about?'

'It has been more than a month since Abbu jaan passed away and we're all still in mourning.'

Zoya said nothing, fully aware that her uncle had bottled up his bitterness and rancour for years, and that it would all come out on this day.

'If only you were here taking care of him that day, Zoya, he wouldn't have lost his life,' and there it was.

'And you wouldn't have had to put on this bereaved act today,' she snapped.

'I am not putting on an act,' he said belligerently.

'Oh, really? During all these years, you just visited him to get his signatures on cheques, as far as I'm aware. And then you started forging his signature, right?'

'I don't know what you're talking about, Zoya,' he denied heatedly, 'and I am not here to argue with you. I am my father's only son and the rightful heir to everything that my father had.'

'And who inherits the responsibilities, duties and liabilities that have accumulated since the time you left?'

He leaned close to Zoya and she could smell his fetid breath, 'I always told your mother that you would make a better politician than a singer. Your debating skills were always phenomenal and you won every argument.'

'What's your point, Mamu?' Zoya asked in a tired voice.

'I am trying to say that this is the law and you can't win with your nonsensical speeches. Business is always dirty, so take my advice and don't get involved in it.'

'And there's one thing Naanu always told me that you were good at,' she retorted.

'What?'

'Nothing,' she scoffed. 'He spent all his life looking for one redeeming quality in you; sadly, his search was in vain.'

'You've got a big mouth, Zoya,' he pushed the chair back with force and stood up. He looked furious.

'Didn't you just tell me that I was good at it?' Zoya smiled dourly and relaxed in her chair.

'Is this how you talk to your elders and betters?'

She shrugged, 'I offered you refreshments but you declined. And, Mamu, as you said, business is dirty.'

She flipped open the folder on the patio table, took out a legal document and handed it over to her Mamu.

'You're five years too late in claiming what could have been yours,' she said. 'You can keep that photocopy,' she said before continuing, 'Naanu transferred this to my name exactly five years ago. Even if I were to die today, I'm certain it's never going to be yours, ever. You had better get off my property now, Mamu,' Zoya commanded coldly.

Mamu jaan stood rooted to the spot in impotent rage. And then, with one final furious glare at her, he stormed out of the house.

This house that Amaan Ali had built with great love and care was the house of his dreams, in which he wanted his children and grandchildren to grow up, thrive and prosper. He had worked hard to build a home that would make his family proud of him, but, as time passed, his dreams shattered one by one: he was heartbroken by his daughter's untimely death. To add to his grief, his son grew indifferent towards him, creating an unfordable chasm. It was Zoya, his granddaughter, who shared his dreams and filled the house with music and happiness. He had hoped to celebrate her wedding with great pomp in this very house.

When the storm eventually broke that evening, Zoya drew the curtains and shuttered the windows, silently vowing to ensure that no storm ever entered her house again.

As if on cue, her cell phone buzzed with a message that read, 'I'm on my way to Pakistan and not to worry, I'll find your address easily given that you're quite the celebrity. Just so you know, biryani is my favourite dish. So, dinner tonight at your place.'

Zoya couldn't help smiling as she reread Kabeer's message. She had been ignoring her phone for the past several days.

'If you're brave enough for my cooking experiments, then sure ☺,' she keyed in and pressed send.

Hundreds of kilometres away, Kabeer smiled as happiness zinged through him.

CHAPTER 18

Just a while ago

Almost a month and a half after the terrorist attack that had shaken both the countries, Arko and Kabeer were practising in the nets of Wankhede Stadium, Mumbai, at the crack of dawn, preparing to return to Pakistan.

This was the second game that was to be held there, with much tighter security arrangements this time. It was an unexpected move that had left many scratching their heads. The media was calling it a highly influenced political move, some people called it a courageous one and most cricket experts were of the opinion that it was foolhardy to the extreme. After what had gone down in Lahore during the last 'friendly' match, many from the team had backed out from another tour in

Pakistan. In their place were eager, younger cricketers, grabbing their first opportunity despite the danger.

Arko was promoted to captain and Kabeer, in his second international match, was declared vice-captain. Kabeer's grandfather wasn't too keen on him going to Pakistan again for a match, but Kabeer was determined to play there despite the circumstances. During the day's practice session, it was clear, however, that Kabeer's heart wasn't in the game.

He missed yet another full toss and was bowled out in the nets.

'What's wrong, Kabeer?' frowned Arko. Like most new captains, he looked understandably worried, especially now that the most junior player in the team had suddenly been promoted to vice-captain.

'Any specific reason you're so tense?' Arko repeated, sipping from his water bottle.

'No, why?'

'Would you like to take a break, maybe?'

'I don't need a break.'

'You do. You're playing random shots. Something's bothering you, I can tell,' Arko sighed. 'I really need you to pay attention to the game. Cover drive attempts at out-swingers, lousy sweeps at full tosses, uppercuts at good length balls,' Arko shook his head and clicked his tongue, 'those are just not on, and we're about to play internationals!' Arko paused for breath, before continuing, 'Is this about what had happened last time? If that's what's bothering you, it's for the good of the team that you leave the squad. That's me as a captain talking. A friend still cares for your sentiments,' Arko grinned.

'No, no. I'm over that, I swear. People really want this match to take place, for their own reasons.'

'It's not about what people want, Kabeer, it's about whether you feel up to it or not. And to be honest, considering the way you're playing, I don't think you're up to it.'

'I've cleared all the required tests by BCCI. What more do I need?'

'Are you mentally fit or still traumatized?'

Unsure of how to respond, Kabeer remained silent.

Arko sighed gustily, 'I'll just wait for you to wrap up, okay? I want to know what's going on in your head.'

'How does it matter?'

'It matters. As a sportsperson, you have to concentrate on the game, no matter what. That's why you're here to play, against all the odds, and still win for your country. For that, you need a friend with whom you can talk.'

'Am I talking to a friend or my captain now?'

'A friend if you're willing to loosen up and talk it out, and a captain if you're going to be the strong, silent type,' Arko replied. Kabeer slapped him. 'What was this for?' Arko demanded, shocked, and looked around to see if anyone else had witnessed the event. But there weren't many people around.

'I don't know, I just wanted to slap someone to take my frustration out,' Kabeer said, chuckling.

'I can get you out of the team for this misconduct, you know that?'

'I slapped my friend, not my captain.' He smiled, and Arko smiled back. 'Do you remember Zoya Malik?' Kabeer asked.

'Who can forget her?' Arko shrugged, 'what's going on, champ?' He folded his hands, waiting for what Kabeer has to say. Kabeer tucked his bat under his arm and went to sit down on a bench behind the nets.

'We met when she was in India and I felt we developed a connection. Her grandfather, Amaan Ali Malik, died that day while she was performing on stage. She started crying and told me how much she was going to miss him as I drove her to the airport. Some journalist even had the audacity to ask her why she had chosen money over her grandfather's death. I could see that that shattered her. I have since left a number of text messages and even called her up, asking about how she's holding up, but she never answers. I'm worried that I read more than I should have into that fleeting encounter.'

Arko drank an entire bottle of mineral water in the silence that followed. 'I know it's a lot to take in for someone who didn't know anything about this. That's why I was keeping it to myself,' Kabeer added.

When Arko continued to remain silent, Kabeer snapped, 'Say something!'

'That's the reason why the management made you vice-captain so soon. You're an opportunist,' Arko chuckled.

'You're making too much of it,' Kabeer said. 'I am worried that's what is impacting my performance,' he added, with a serious expression.

'You know what Kabeer,' Arko said as he adjusted his shoelaces, 'I was always terrified of beamers and yorkers when I was on strike. I've often thrown my wicket out of fear, but then I realized that it's not the yorkers or beamers that got to me, it was my way of dealing with them. The only way to get rid of a phobia is to face one's fears head on. So, I decided at the time to face only yorkers and beamers in my net sessions. Within a month, I had overcome my fears and was even able to laugh at them.' This was a long speech for Arko. 'Message her one last time and do it in style this time.'

Kabeer took out his phone and mulled over what to write. He wasn't too sure about what he was doing, but he typed out his message anyway and paused for some time before pressing send.

'I am on my way to Pakistan and it isn't difficult to find out the address of a celebrity like you. Just so you know, I like biryani more than anything. If you know how to make some, keep it ready. It's going to be dinner tonight at your place.'

CHAPTER 19

April '17

Kabeer was headed towards Bangalore airport that
night pondering the mysterious plane tickets. He
hadn't given it much thought when he came across
the tickets in Mumbai and had flown to Bangalore
on a whim. When he realized that it had all been
in vain, he felt incredibly stupid to have acted so
impulsively.

He grew suspicious when he found another
e-ticket, this time, to Delhi. He realized that someone
had deliberately set up a wild goose chase for him and
Kabeer had a niggling suspicion that it wasn't Zoya.
Nevertheless, he found himself aboard the next flight
to Delhi. This felt like his only chance and he didn't
dare give up, however futile it seemed.

Kabeer felt foolish like he was being stalked by some prankster who could read his mind and seemed to anticipate his every move. He didn't know if he was just being paranoid, but he had been travelling for almost five hours now and the trauma of the previous day's events only added to this phobia. Exhausted but determined to leave for Delhi immediately, he reached the airport at 6.30 a.m. As luck would have it, the next flight to Delhi wasn't until 9.30 in the morning.

Fatigued and miserable, he sank into a seat in the lounge. His mobile was running low on battery and he wondered how to kill time until it was time for take-off. He wasn't aware exactly when he drifted off to sleep.

The next thing he knew was opening his eyes to the bustle of people in the airport. He reached for his phone to look at the time, but its battery had died by then. The airport clock on the electronic airport schedule panel read 10.30 a.m. He had missed his flight by a whole hour! Panicking, he rushed towards the airlines counter.

'I missed my flight, AE-520.'

'Please wait a moment, sir, let us check the details.'

'What "details" are you cross-checking? I am here and I am telling you that I missed it!' Kabeer shouted.

'I'm sorry for the inconvenience, sir,' the calm and immaculately groomed woman manning the ground staff desk replied, 'but we called you at 8.30 a.m., 8.35

a.m., 8.45 a.m. and 9.05 a.m., but the call wouldn't connect.'

'You could've at least announced my name.'

'Sir, this is a silent airport. Announcements aren't allowed here. There's nothing more we can do to help you out,' she said coldly. 'If you're done, we're next,' interrupted the middle-aged woman behind him in the queue. Kabeer didn't budge.

'When is the next flight to Delhi?' Kabeer asked.

'At noon, but it's full, so you can take the flight after that at 1.30 p.m.'

'Okay, I'll take it. Please book a ticket for me.'

'Sir, would you like to book a plus ticket for yourself? You can get your luggage on priority and also a seat with extra leg space.'

'No. A normal seat will do.'

'Aisle, middle or window, sir?'

'Anything will do.'

'Do you want vegetarian or non-vegetarian food, sir?' The woman behind him was growing restless and fidgeting incessantly.

'Vegetarian food,' Kabeer's dwindling patience was hanging by a thread.

He was finally handed his ticket. It was going to be a nearly three-hour wait before he could board.

'Thank you for booking a ticket with Fly airlines, we hope you have a good journey with us,' the woman chirped with a plastic smile, 'Fly high.'

Kabeer stared unseeingly at a TV screen for a while until a line, repeatedly scrolling at the bottom of the screen, caught his eye: #shameonkabeer. A footage of him attacking the reporter was played over and over again and even though the volume was on mute, he could make out by the grim expression of the newsreader and the tagline that it was acrimonious condemnation. He quietly walked away from the curious stares and whispers around him.

He slipped into a bookstore and hid himself between the shelves. Casually browsing through the books around him, his eyes suddenly locked on a book. It was an autobiography written by Amaan Malik, published recently, with a full body portrait of him on the cover. Needing a distraction from the disturbing stream of thoughts running through his mind, he decided to buy it. He remained engrossed in the book even as he landed in Delhi at 4.45 p.m. and stayed back in the airport to finish the last page.

My daughter, Mariam, was crying. The shock of seeing my beloved child in pain, both physical and emotional, was seared into my brain. Her eyes were bottomless pools of distress—an expression that I had never seen before.

It was late. A little past two in the morning. I was flying to India for my concert and was on my way to the airport.

My princess was in a salwar suit that seemed to have been ripped in some sort of a scuffle. I realized that I had been living in a fool's paradise about my child's marital bliss and had failed to see her marriage crumble, crushing her beneath its ruins. The scales fell from my eyes at her revelations and I was shocked to learn of the abusive relationship that my daughter had been suffering at the hands of her husband, Danish, the son of an influential politician. She had silently borne his ill-treatment for over a decade, but today, when Danish's inebriated violence extended to her daughter, she fled from her farcical marriage with her child. I was glad that she came to me that night and I embraced my weeping daughter.

I telephoned Danish and made it abundantly clear that Mariam wasn't ever going to return to him and that he would rue the day if he attempted to even approach her or Zoya.

I ensured that my daughter never wept again. Unfortunately, cancer raised its ugly head a few years later. Zoya was young and I did my utmost to hide the inevitable doom that hung over our heads. One fateful night, she overheard a conversation between Mariam and me. Zoya understood that her mother wasn't long for this world, but she rode out that storm like a stalwart. I realized to my immense pride and joy exactly how brave and strong young Zoya was.

Not a day passes when I don't think of you, my loveliest daughter. You left too early and I am ashamed of being a father who couldn't help you survive, but trust me, I did everything that I could to save you, my angel. Of all the promises I made to you, that was the only one I broke. Please forgive me if you can.

There is a promise I would like you to make, though. You'll wait for me until I reach you and embrace you again, my love, because life without you isn't going to be a life worth living. The day I leave this world for my heavenly abode is the day that I will finally sleep peacefully and sleep forever. I want my daughter to feel secure in my arms and this time, as I hold you, I promise to not let you slip away as I did the last time. I hope and believe that this time I am able to protect you from demons—living or dead. Your old father misses you a lot, princess. See you in heaven.'

Kabeer hadn't realized that he'd got emotional; as he was closing the book, two drops of tear fell on the last page.

CHAPTER 20

July '16

Staring out of the window that night, Zoya thought of Kabeer. Since her grandfather's death, she hadn't been able to talk to him. She had replayed those conversations in her head, the things they had talked about when they had met in India. She looked at the watch and checked his live location on WhatsApp. She dialled his number but hung up as soon as a cab pulled up in the portico.

Kabeer smiled and waved at her from a distance. Zoya greeted him with a hug at the door.

'Returning to this country after what you faced last time requires a lot of courage.'

'Not when a person who lives beyond the border stops responding to your calls and messages.'

'I was having a hard time dealing with Naanu's death.'

'Which was why I was all the more concerned. I needed to know that you were coping.'

Zoya smiled, 'Having you here definitely makes me feel better. Thanks for coming.'

'I am here for a while so thank me later.'

'How long?'

'I am here for about fifteen days and I am going to meet you every day to make sure that you're doing okay,' Kabeer said. 'Believe me, you need someone to be pushy or else you will not know when to switch the cooker off when you're making biryani for your guest,' he added with a wink.

Zoya sniffed the air and realized that something was burning. Alarmed, she ran into the kitchen and opened the cooker. The biryani could no longer be termed biryani. She felt devastated and cursed herself.

Kabeer burst out laughing.

'Are you laughing at me?' scowled Zoya. She did her best to resuscitate the biryani, but it was too late.

'Of course not,' Kabeer denied stoutly, 'I wouldn't dare.' He helpfully opened the windows and turned on the exhaust fan to vent out the smell of burnt food. 'Is this how you welcome guests from India?'

'I think I have a better way to respect an Indian guest. Let me call the police and tell them that there's an Indian intruder who has broken into my house and has kept me as a hostage.'

'No doubt you Pakistanis are so good at lies,' Kabeer said jokingly.

'Would you like to throw some light upon our lies?' Zoya frowned.

'The first one: Kashmir is ours,' he replied.

'Okay, but Azad Kashmir is ours,' Zoya aggressively counter-attacked him.

'So what? You guys have taken that from us. Don't forget that we captured Lahore as well in 1965.'

'Let's not get into that. We have also done many things that deserve accolades.'

'Would you mind refreshing my memory a bit? Winning in the Champions trophy finals?'

'That too.'

'Come on, don't behave like Bangladesh now.' They both burst out laughing.

'So, what brought you here?'

'Two reasons: a cricket match and to see you.' Kabeer glanced at Amaan Ali's portrait on the wall.

'Oh, I thought you just came to meet me!' Zoya said jestingly.

'That's another truth,' Kabeer said seriously. He didn't seem to realize that Zoya was mocking him.

'Liar.'

'Many Indian players dropped out at the last minute because of the dangers involved in playing in Pakistan.

I could've opted out too had I not had a second motive to come here.'

'Did you come all the way to Lahore from Karachi just to see me?'

'Do you even have to ask?'

'Because there's always a motive behind everything.'

'Would you believe me if I said I had no ulterior motive?'

'Absolutely not,' Zoya retorted.

'That's the problem with you Pakistanis. If I was from China, you would've believed me in an instant.'

'Is this prime time, Kabeer?'

'Not at all.'

'Then talk to my hand,' she said sarcastically.

'Zoya, at times, we just do some things because they're a no-brainer. I sincerely wanted to come and see you because I was worried about you.'

'You got worried for me within just two short meetings?'

'I couldn't wait forever to start getting worried about you.'

'There's a reason you're from India.'

'And what's that?'

'No matter what, you guys are always good at convincing.'

'Enough with the India–Pakistan thing.'

'You started!'

'For a change,' Kabeer said and laughed.

'Fuck you! I am glad my biryani got burnt.'

'It's not too late for the wine bottles to be opened though,' he added.

'I am so happy that you came. You're a darling.'

Kabeer poured out wine into the glasses and they continued to chat, sometimes seriously and sometimes, not so seriously, until the pizza arrived. Zoya collected the boxes and placed them on the enormous dining table.

It was as she prised open the first box that she noticed a folded piece of paper taped to the side. Confused, she carefully unfolded the note:

'THANKS FOR GETTING KABEER BACK IN PAKISTAN; THIS TIME HE WILL NOT GO BACK ALIVE.'

Zoya stared at the message for several minutes before quickly running to the door to see if the delivery boy was still there. He was gone.

'Is everything all right?'

'Yes. Absolutely,' Zoya quickly hid the piece of paper behind her back.

'You look worried.'

'I'm sharing a drink with an Indian, I have to be worried.'

'Not as dangerous as drinking a toast with a Pakistani in Pakistan.'

'I'm gonna ensure that this time around you do trust a Pakistani in Pakistan,' Zoya said with a sad smile.

Kabeer looked at her enigmatically.

Zoya took a deep breath and sliced the pizza into sectors.

CHAPTER 21

April '17

It was a little past 5.30 p.m. when he arrived at Taj hotel in Delhi. By now, Kabeer knew the drill to this wild goose chase. He asked to be given room 701, the room he had shared with Zoya the previous year.

'Sorry, sir. That room is occupied,' the pretty young receptionist apologized.

'How is that possible?' Kabeer asked, confused.

'Did you book it in advance?' she asked.

'No. Someone else has been doing it on my behalf,' Kabeer replied hesitantly.

'In that case, could you check with them, or settle for another room tonight and we'll provide you with room 701 as soon as it's vacated tomorrow morning?'

'Is any other room available on the same floor?'

'Umm, 702 is across the corridor. Will that do?'

Kabeer nodded. As he went through the formalities of being booked into 702, the elevator doors pinged and the person who emerged dropped a room key card on the reception desk, murmuring, 'I'll be back in a bit.' Kabeer glanced at the card casually and froze. Printed across the key card in bold black letters was the number 701.

His desire to get to the bottom of the mystery trumped Kabeer's scruples. His heart started racing as he realized he could actually make this work. He had to get into room 701 and that too, by tonight.

'I have to go out now. Can you hand over my room key to my manager who will be here in about two hours?' Kabeer asked the receptionist.

'I'm very sorry, sir. I clock out at 6 p.m., but I can ensure that my colleague who will take over after my shift gives your manager the key card.'

'Aah, don't worry about it. I'll give him a call and ask him to come to the room directly.'

The bellboy picked up his duffel bag and propped the lift door open. Kabeer walked in.

It was 5.42 p.m. by now. Kabeer noticed that the CCTV camera in the corridor changed direction every thirty seconds.

He showered and changed and then paced in his room for about ten minutes. At exactly 5.59 p.m., he rode the elevator to the lobby and handed his key card to the smiling receptionist who was winding up for the day.

'Have a nice evening, sir,' she said politely, accepting his key card, 'see you tomorrow.'

Kabeer quickly walked out of the hotel. He had to steel himself to execute his plan. It wasn't as if he had practiced breaking in before. Anything could go wrong, and he couldn't afford for that to happen.

He watched from a safe distance as the night shift employee took over. He waited for just about ten seconds before approaching the reception desk.

'Key, please? 701?' Kabeer asked, pretending to be deeply immersed in a phone call.

'Here's your room access, sir. Have a good evening,' the new receptionist on duty said.

The adrenaline of this escapade thrummed through Kabeer's veins filling him with a strange exhilaration, not unlike the kind he experienced on the cricket field when about to face an unknown bowler. As soon as he arrived on the seventh floor he had one eye monitoring the movements of the CCTV camera. The moment it turned the other way would be his cue to enter room 701. He stood in the lobby, pretending to speak on the phone while he waited.

The camera finally turned away and he quickly ran to 701, swiped the access card, entered the room and slammed the door shut.

He stood panting against the door. He didn't quickly began searching the room for clues of her whereabouts. He opened a drawer excitedly but found it empty. He opened another drawer and rummaged inside but couldn't find anything out of the ordinary, except the occupant's cell phone charger and spectacle case. He hurriedly searched the wardrobe, the other drawers and the wooden racks but found nothing. He sat on the edge of the bed feeling disheartened. Was this a dead end? He prepared to sneak out of the room and waited for the CCTV camera to rotate. He had set his watch timer to the camera and knew exactly when it would turn away, and successfully dodged its line of view as he left the room.

He rode the elevator down and stormed over to the reception, looking furious.

'You are so careless! I was busy on a call and mistakenly said room 701 and without even checking the records, you gave me the key card! What if I had been a burglar?'

'I'm extremely sorry, sir. I assure you that it was unintentional and won't happen again,' the receptionist stammered nervously.

'Give me my key card to room 702 now,' Kabeer demanded, feeling sorry for the hapless receptionist. This time, the receptionist made sure to check the computer's records before handing over the card to Kabeer.

As Kabeer reached his room, he pondered the trail of clues that had been left for him. If Zoya was indeed the person behind them, why hadn't she just messaged or called him directly? Why this elaborate roundaboutation? If it was someone else playing a prank, what was the motive?

As Kabeer mulled over these questions, he poured himself a glass of wine. One glass led to another and soon, Kabeer was fast asleep in a chair on the balcony, too tired and drunk to make it into bed.

His duffel bag hadn't been unpacked and he decided to abandon his quest. He picked up his bag and clicked the door shut behind him. As he turned to head down the carpeted corridor to the lift he glanced at the room numbers 701 and 702 on the doors, and a faint memory stirred. He remembered that last year too the hotel had provided him with room 702's keys as the people who were in 701 had extended their stay. He ran back to his room and checked the drawers. Sure enough, there it was. Another e-ticket in Zoya's name. This time, although the name and timings were written on it, the destination and flight number were scored out manually with a pen. He flipped it over and saw a paper stuck on the other side:

'I can't wait to see you.'

Kabeer almost dropped the ticket in shock. This wasn't Zoya's handwriting, it belonged to someone he knew very well.

It was his own.

CHAPTER 22

April '17

He stared at the sentence. It was six in the morning
and he was still groggy. He remembered writing a love
letter to Zoya. It looked like the last line of the letter
had been torn off and pasted here.

'I can't wait to see you.'

He wanted to scream in frustration. The only way
he could get closure was by going to Pakistan—an
impossibility at this juncture because (a) there were no
cricket tournaments underway in that country (b) the
political climate between the two countries was overcast
and (c) his past relationship with Zoya was common
knowledge, so he would be refused a travel visa.

He looked at the e-ticket again and tried to figure
out the next clue. He remembered visiting Mumbai,

Bangalore and Delhi for Zoya's concert tour and if that sequence had anything to do with this trail, he knew which city he had to visit next—Lahore. This entire exercise now felt like a game of treasure hunt. The treasure of his life, Zoya.

He googled the flight number 6E-829. It belonged to Fly Air, the airline that operated between Delhi and Lahore. He was certain that someone—perhaps Zoya, perhaps not—wanted him to visit Lahore.

He was having trouble processing all these conundrums, but the thought of meeting Zoya again galvanized him. A part of him refuted the idea that Zoya would play such a cruel trick on him. He poured himself one last glass of wine to help him cogitate and soon emptied the whole bottle. He thought about the letter that he had once written to Zoya. He had been in Pakistan when he had decided to declare his love for Zoya in the most romantic way he could think of—a handwritten letter.

Dear Zoya,

How weird is life? Never in my wildest dreams did I imagine myself visiting Pakistan or using Pakistan Post to send you a letter. A mere verbal expression would not do justice to the depth of my feelings for you; therefore, I have decided to write a letter and document my love for you. It is crucial to express oneself rather than bottle up emotions waiting for just the right moment. I hope that you will read every word in this letter with the same sentiment that I've written them.

I fell in love with you long before we met in India. The moment I saw you on one of those huge billboards, I knew I wanted to spend the rest of my life with you. I am someone who never makes split-second decisions, but I was sure about my feelings for you from the word go.

Because even after knowing you for only a few months, I can hear the sound of our laughter together; I can see myself growing old with you, but most importantly, I can hear the words you would probably never say and I hope that you too someday feel the same.

As I write this letter to you, I hope that you would not just read it but read every word with the same sentiment that I've written them with, because if they can't tell you my feelings, trust me, nothing else will.

I know the challenge I face. Our nations are at loggerheads. Our people might or might not be too fond of each other and our love story, if there ever would be, might keep fluctuating with what's happening at the border but I believe that there is a way out. I'm also aware that your grandfather always wanted peace between our countries, which gives me hope.

We have heard many stories of hatred between India and Pakistan but, for a change, let's talk about love. Let us forget that we're on opposite sides of the battle line because I love you so much that these borders don't matter any more.

What matters are your feelings. Do you also see a forever with me just as I do? I promise to be your Pakistan if you are ready to be my India when in need.

I love you more with each passing second. My heart races as I write this little note, but I am glad that I wrote it after all. I will be leaving Pakistan in a little bit and am not sure when I will be back. All I'm trying to say is, 'I can't wait to see you.'

Kabeer

CHAPTER 23

July '16

That night, after a few drinks, Kabeer stayed awake all night, admiring Zoya's incredible beauty. How easy it had been to fall in love with her!

A breeze drifted in through the open window and gently caressed her hair. Her skin, like alabaster in the moonlight, was a perfect foil for the sweep of her long, dark eyelashes as she slept peacefully, her beautiful lips softly parted. Kabeer felt all his doubts and anxieties evaporate. If someday Zoya accepted his proposal and agreed to marry him, Kabeer was certain he would weep with joy.

Wait. Was it too early to think that far? How did that even matter as long as these thoughts warmed his soul with contentment?

The breeze gradually picked up and the rustling of the leaves seemed to herald a beautiful wind of change. He wondered whether she would believe him if he declared his feelings for her. Would she reciprocate his passion someday?

The duvet rose and fell rhythmically with her breathing and then, as if she had sensed his gaze, Zoya's eyes fluttered open, and they stared into each other's eyes. Kabeer was unaware of a stupid, lopsided smile spreading across his lips as he continued looking at her.

'I'm sorry,' said Kabeer.

'I should apologize,' she said, her voice husky with sleep. 'I fell asleep with a guest at home. How rude am I?' Zoya sat up, yawned and stretched. 'Would you like some tea? Green or regular?' she called out as she went into the kitchen.

'An . . . any . . . thing,' Kabeer stammered, following her into the kitchen. 'Um . . . I'm sorry about earlier. You looked extraordinarily beautiful as you slept, I didn't mean to wake you.'

Zoya put the kettle on and turned to face him. She drew closer and looked into his eyes. Kabeer realized he was holding his breath.

'You have such beautiful eyes, Kabeer,' she said softly.

'Do I?' he murmured.

Zoya raised herself on her toes. Their lips met and they kissed slowly, languorously. They could hear each other's breathing.

A dam seemed to break and their hands seemed to move with minds of their own, quickly unbuttoning their clothes until Kabeer's hands held her smooth, bare back, pressing her body tight against himself. He kissed her swan-like neck and Zoya balled her fists to control the urge to rake her nails on Kabeer's muscled back. She ripped off Kabeer's shirt and he immediately flipped her around.

Their love-making was feral and passionate with each trying to gain control over the other on the couch by mounting the other. Whence Zoya threw her head back gasping, Kabeer saw a shadow outside the window and a camera flashed, blinding him momentarily.

'What was that?'

'Someone's outside taking pictures of us!'

Zoya crouched down into the couch. Kabeer rushed to the window just in time to see a hooded figure vault over the fence in the backyard and run away. Zoya called her manager and publicity team and told them about the incident. An hour went by as they waited on tenterhooks for the scandalizing pictures to go viral on the Internet. They were not sure if the mystery cameraman had actually been able to capture any concrete evidence of their liaison.

'Zoya, let's hope for the best now,' Kabeer murmured, his warm hand covered hers. 'There's no point in worrying ourselves sick now, we just have to wait and watch,' he stroked her hair comfortingly.

Zoya sighed, 'You're probably right.' She kissed his cheek, 'Just so you know, I plan to join you for the rest of your tour. But, this time around, you get to see my country through my eyes and when you go back home, you'll have only good memories of Pakistan. We leave in fifteen minutes.'

CHAPTER 24

July '16

'Whatever be the outcome of this match, the spirit of the sport will prevail,' an anchor proclaimed as the crowd erupted with cheers.

Three days after the Indian team reached the National Cricket Stadium, Karachi, escorted by a horde of security personnel bristling with weapons and hand-held shields, both inside and outside the stadium, to prevent a repeat attack, the T-20 match was all set to begin.

India won the toss and opted to bat first. After congregating for the national anthem, the players dispersed to their positions and Kabeer went in to bat along with Shaurya, another strong opener. He glanced at the pavilion and spotted Zoya in the crowd. She blew him a kiss.

Over the last three days, Kabeer and Zoya's romance had become the hottest topic for the media. Indo–Pak friendship had new poster children—Kabeer and Zoya. Some said they were dating since they had last met during the friendly match in Pakistan; others claimed that they were getting engaged soon and some were of the opinion that it was just a phase and would soon be over. None of this worried Kabeer, though. Something else gave him sleepless nights.

'5 . . . 4 . . . 3 . . . 2 . . . 1 . . . Kabeer on strike will face one the deadliest of bowlers in the world, Nadeem. The countdown begins!' came the voice of an Indian commentator as Kabeer skilfully placed the ball for a quick four to the off side, inaugurating the innings in style.

The match grew heated as the Pakistani team failed to come up with an adequate response to Kabeer and Shaurya's aggressive batting. India was sixty-three for no loss after six overs. Every time Kabeer hit a sixer or boundary, the videographers deliberately zoomed in on Zoya's reaction in the stands as she clapped and punched the air. Kabeer completed his quickest fifty in just twenty-three balls. He kissed his bat and pointed it towards Zoya triumphantly.

When drinks were served to both the teams, Pakistan's captain, Nadeem, approached Kabeer and asked, 'So, how was your exploration here?'

'I haven't really seen much of Pakistan,' Kabeer smiled. 'Not enough time.'

'I wasn't talking about Pakistan. I was talking about Zoya; you seem to have explored her quite a bit. What was better? The north or the south—'

Kabeer furiously launched himself at Nadeem, before Shaurya, who was at opposite end of the pitch, ran over to hold him back.

'You come here and fuck our girl, do you think we'd keep quiet?' Nadeem shouted, his face red with rage.

'You bastard! It's your girl who spread her legs!' Shaurya hollered at him, which didn't help at all and Kabeer glared at Shaurya.

'Who cares who did what first? He's well aware that she's an heiress,' Nadeem jeered from a distance. Kabeer charged at him again, but this time the fielders and wicketkeepers converged along with Shaurya to form a wall between him and Nadeem, while a couple of the senior Pakistani team members tried to calm Nadeem down.

When the match resumed, everything seemed normal on the surface. However, a taut tension stretched between Kabeer and Nadeem. Nadeem bowled an excellent in-swinger that hit the middle stump and Kabeer was clean bowled. Nadeem jumped up and down with unholy glee, gesturing aggressively at Kabeer, who bent his head, keeping a tight lid on his rage.

As Kabeer returned to the pavilion, Arko emerged with Kishor, a debutant. He passed Kabeer with a bitter look that spoke volumes.

'What happened there?' asked Zoya, looking anxiously at Kabeer, who, still seething, shouldered his way into the dressing room.

'Nothing.'

'It didn't look like "nothing" from where I stood,' she snapped.

'How does it even matter?' Kabeer asked tiredly as he tucked his bat under his arm.

'So, whatever happened there doesn't matter to you? Do you think people will just forget what you did today on the field?'

'And you think what Nadeem did was fair?'

'You were the one who attacked him, not vice versa.'

'After what he said about you, I'm only sorry that I didn't get to beat him to a pulp.'

'In a match that was a peace deal, your only regret is not hitting someone,' Zoya said sarcastically, 'that's fair.' She clicked her tongue and shook her head sorrowfully at Kabeer, 'such a shame.'

'Why do I get the feeling that this is a Pakistani talking to an Indian?' Kabeer asked with a sidelong glance at her.

'There was much more to this match than just nations, Kabeer,' Zoya sighed. Kabeer chuckled.

Zoya realized for the first time that she didn't like the sound of his laugh.

'Wearing a Pakistani T-shirt, cheering for an Indian guy and supporting a Pakistani cricketer who slut-shamed you,' Kabeer mocked her. 'Do you still think I shouldn't have reacted the way I did? Sorry to disappoint you, ma'am,' Kabeer walked past her and into the dressing room where his team was waiting for him.

'You know, Kabeer, there's a difference between aggression and being plain dumb on the field?' the coach said expressionlessly.

'And you know pretty much everything that happened out there?' Kabeer challenged, flinging his bat into the equipment trunk and slamming down the lid. He sat down on the bench and unbuckled his batting gear.

'I know what people will think when they watch the reruns of the footage on TV. And what will the headlines be—"A Star is Born" or "A Brat with a Bat"?' the coach replied stoically.

'Wow! And here I was thinking that it was hard enough convincing the Pakistanis about my integrity, but my own coach has labelled me a brat.'

'I think you've been out in the sun too long today, kid. You need to lie down and take it easy,' the coach replied, patting Kabeer on the shoulder.

Arko looked uncomfortable at the crease initially but, as the game progressed, India comfortably secured 183 for five wickets in the stipulated twenty overs before they dispersed for a break. Kabeer remained dourly, dwelling on the confrontation on the pitch. He looked around for Zoya, but she was nowhere to be seen.

Completing the innings and making a mature half-century for India, Arko walked triumphantly back to the pavilion and immediately started issuing instructions to his team.

'Shaurya, you're at the slip; Raman, you'll start the bowling because the ball is spinning a fair bit; and Raman-Ricky, you cover the first four overs,' Arko had all the flair and panache of a skipper and everybody automatically looked up to him.

'Arko, where do I field?' Kabeer asked.

Arko avoiding his eyes. 'You're injured for the next few matches, including this one,' he declared and left the pavilion with the team.

CHAPTER 25

July '16

We're all destined to play certain roles in our own love stories. Sometimes we find ourselves playing the role of a friend who supports the other even when they are wrong. At other times we want a friend understand our angst even when the whole world turns against us and stand by us in the teeth of opposition. If that doesn't happen, we begin to doubt ourselves.

Three days after India A won the first T-20 by fifty-three runs, the evening skies lowered in Multan where the second T-20 international match was scheduled to take place.

'After a huge win over Pakistan in the last match, Pakistan is all set to take on India today! The conditions already seem to be favouring Pakistan as India's star player and vice-captain, Kabeer, is still injured and unavailable to play for this match,' declared former Pakistani captain Jalal Maqsood as he gestured towards the grounds, beaming into the camera.

'The skies are leaden and a storm seems to be brewing. But even if it holds off, a storm is sure to break out on the grounds of Multan today,' countered the Indian commentator beside Jalal.

Tension crackled in the air like never before. This series was clearly anything but peaceful.

Pakistan won the toss and elected to bat first. Kabeer, ensconced in a plush sports café, drained his cup of coffee and watched the match begin.

'Just because I tried protecting my girl on the field, you ejected me from the team,' Kabeer recalled his conversation with Arko from the previous night.

'I had to,' Arko replied.

Kabeer squeezed his eyes shut for a moment. Arko was right. His behaviour on the field had been unacceptable.

'That wasn't your call to make. I was your captain and you should have consulted me.'

'You had to have been there for that, Arko. I'm a player and what was I to do if not express myself?'

'There's a difference between "expressing yourself" and "losing your rag" when the opposing team needles you. You should have just ignored him.'

'I don't agree, Arko.'

'You may think that you could make a place for yourself in my team with this attitude, but I don't agree,' Arko snapped.

Kabeer didn't like the way Arko was talking to him. He was deeply hurt to learn that Zoya had also taken the same stand as Arko on this issue. Broken-hearted, Kabeer moved out that night. A maelstrom of emotions roiled within him—anger and guilt, distress and confusion.

A burst of cheering from the people in the pub broke into Kabeer's ruminations and he realized that the first over had bagged fifteen runs with no loss of wickets.

This wasn't probably the greatest start to an innings, but it was a start nevertheless. Kabeer was glad to have the corner seat, probably the only place in the pub that was out of everyone else's line of view. Kabeer observed the crowd. He knew that the Pakistanis were just as gung ho as the Indians were about cricket. Pakistan scored ninety-three runs for the loss of one wicket in the first ten overs and the crowd jumped up gleefully, clapping and shouting slogans decrying the challenging team.

'*Ek do teen char*, India *harega har baar*,' someone shouted and everyone joined him.

'*Koi na sehan kar paayega* Pakistan *ki maar ko, kisi ka balla nahi chalega, kya* Shaurya *kya* Arko?'

another enthusiastic fan yelled out and people burst into laughter.

The Pakistani batsmen were hitting the Indian bowlers ruthlessly. The Indian players were desperately fielding at the far edges of the ground and every experiment, every bowler and every strategy that India came up with failed, as Pakistan's team ended up posting a huge score of 195 runs for the loss of four wickets at the end of twenty overs—their highest-ever score against India.

During the ten-minute break when the people in the pub retreated into groups to discuss the match, Kabeer's thoughts wandered to his last conversation with Zoya. They were sitting across from each other during dinner at an exclusive restaurant.

'I know that this issue has been preying on your mind,' Kabeer said.

'Someone has to think about it,' Zoya shrugged, unwilling to get dragged into another wrangle about the rights and wrongs of it.

'What about my perspective?'

'Your captain has already expelled you for the rest of the tour, so none of this matters any more,' she sighed, and after a pause continued, 'you've got to be mature about it, accept your mistake and make a formal apology.'

'That's easy to say for a person who has known me for only two months,' Kabeer pushed his plate away.

'I stood up for you and defended your honour,' bitterness had crept into his voice, 'and yet, you took the side of your fellow Pakistani.'

'It's not about him being a Pakistani,' protested Zoya, 'it's about professionalism.'

'And who are you to lecture me on professionalism?' Kabeer frowned angrily.

Zoya flared up. 'Someone who had to perform live while her grandfather breathed his last on his deathbed. Tell me about professionalism.' She pushed her chair back as she said this and flounced out, leaving Kabeer alone at the table.

The Pakistani team entered the ground and a loud cheer in the pub broke Kabeer's reverie yet again. Cheers for India, however, didn't last for more than two overs as India lost three crucial wickets for just eleven runs in two overs, although Arko remained at the crease.

Someone shouted, '*Paanch, che, saat, aath*, India *ki lag gayi waat*.' Kabeer felt his patience rapidly slipping. As he rose to vent his spleen, a commentator exclaimed, 'And here we go! Arko has hit Nadeem for what is the longest six of the tournament, 103 metres!'

The mood in the pub instantly underwent a change, as everybody waited in pin-drop silence for what was to follow. Twenty minutes later, eyes were still glued to the screen in worry. India had completed seventy-five runs for the loss of three wickets in eight overs.

When India's score stood at 137 with the loss of three wickets in thirteen overs, another wicket fell and the room erupted with hoots again. Kabeer, unable to contain his frustration, pounded the table. Every head swivelled in his direction and then everybody went slack-jawed as they realized who he was.

'Well, well, well. And who have we here?' a stranger jeered.

'That was some show you put on, didn't you? And you have the nerve to show up in a public place,' another taunted.

People eyeballed Kabeer in the uncomfortable lull that ensued. A buzz slowly began, soft murmurs at first that gradually grew louder as everybody hurled abuses at him. Kabeer stood still, while the waiters and managers of the establishment did their best to placate everybody before the mood combusted into a riot and destroyed their shop.

At that moment, Arko hit two consecutive sixes from Nadeem's bowling to raise the Indian score to 149 for the loss of four wickets in 13.2 overs. The commentators' hysterical verbosity distracted the palpable animosity. Kabeer silently congratulated and thanked Arko.

Attention oscillated between Kabeer and the TV screen. The match arrived at a very interesting equation with India needing fourteen runs off the last over. Arko returned to the pavilion after making a remarkable ninety-seven runs in forty-two deliveries.

After experimenting with various permutations and combinations of fielding and shots, it was the last ball and India needed three runs. Everyone in the coffee shop, including the waiters and managers, watched with bated breath, ignoring Kabeer. The bowler bowled quickly, the ball veered wide off the stumps and the wicketkeeper missed fielding it. Taking advantage of the hiatus, the Indian batsmen quickly stole two runs and completed the match with a tie.

Kabeer punched the air triumphantly. Heads turned towards him again. High on victory, he smirked, 'We still lead the series with 1:0.'

That did it. All hell broke loose and someone thumped Kabeer from behind. He spun around and punched the man's face. The employees desperately tried to restore peace and order. They formed a protective circle around Kabeer and yelled at everyone to stop. Meanwhile, Kabeer fell into a scuffle with the man who had hit him. Both rolled on the floor, jabbing at each other wildly. A police siren wailed in the distance and as expected, cops barged in within a few minutes. Kabeer and his attacker stood apart, panting. Quickly and efficiently the constabulary secured the attacker and several other miscreants who were busy beating each other up.

Kabeer suddenly noticed Zoya. She was standing quietly by the door, observing the scene. Kabeer had assumed that she had returned to Lahore.

'What's your name?' the long arm of the law demanded of Kabeer.

'That's none of your business,' Zoya cut in coldly. 'You know who he is and you also know who hit whom.'

'But we need to interrogate him, ma'am,' bleated the policeman.

'You may have heard my father's name. MLA Danish. Would you like to speak to him?' Zoya asked disdainfully and swept out, towing Kabeer along.

CHAPTER 26

July '16

'What are you still doing here?' Kabeer asked.

Zoya merely gestured to him to get in the car. She drove in silence for a while.

At long last, she sighed, 'What happened in there?'

'They did something they shouldn't have,' Kabeer replied mutinously.

'And what was that?'

'They cursed the Indians and my teammates.'

'And you decided to go all Sunny Deol and beat up the Pakistanis in Pakistan?' Zoya raised an eyebrow in incredulity.

'Oh, *main nikla, gaddi leke,*' Kabeer grinned unrepentantly.

'Fuck you and fuck your gaddi!' Zoya snapped and jammed the brakes. She turned in her seat to face him, 'I fell in love with your sincerity, but I don't see that any more.'

'Says the person who abandoned me in a country that's baying for my blood. How ironic is that?'

'Don't be so melodramatic, Kabeer. Nobody wants you dead.'

'First, a terrorist attack and then some random people ganging up on me in a café. What would you term those? Yes, no one is after my life and I am so glad that you ran away from everything that happened.'

'You could've called me to apologize.'

'If you're dead set on receiving an apology from me, you will have to wait, my love, until I do make a mistake.'

'So, you still don't accept you were in the wrong to attempt aggravated assault in full public glare, for the world to see.'

'All the more because you've already judged and gaoled me and thrown away the key.'

'Why are you so obstinate?'

'Zoya, I can't help it if you aren't familiar with the term "logic". And I can't be talking whims and fancies all the time.'

'You're crossing the line, Kabeer.'

'And the people who hit me didn't, right?'

'Did I say that?'

'But you meant that.'

'I think there's a problem with the way your brain functions.'

'So you accept that I have one despite the media's label on me.'

Zoya frowned as Kabeer continued his rant, 'All your country has is a bunch of losers who do nothing but crib. I suppose your grandfather was no different.'

Zoya was stunned at this low blow. They glared at each other for a while, till tears flooded down her cheeks.

His words had pierced her heart; they were the ultimate betrayal. She was heartbroken. Her eyes glared at him but her tears recited the tale of a broken heart. She wanted to yell at him, but was rendered speechless.

Kabeer got out of the car and slammed the door shut.

Despite the hurt, Zoya could hear a little voice urging her to warn Kabeer that it wasn't safe for him to be outside. But she was fuming at his crass insensitivity. She buried her head in her arms against the steering wheel and cried.

Why was this happening to her? She knew she deserved better than this. Why was Kabeer suddenly acting so strange?

She sat up sniffling and reached for the ignition when something tiny whizzed past the window and hit the wing mirror. Confused, Zoya rolled down her window. It was a small dart with a tiny suction cup at one end and a scroll of paper at the other. She plucked the dart from the mirror and undid the string that held the scrap of paper, scanning her surroundings to see where it had come from. Had someone deliberately aimed it for her car? But there was no one in sight. Unfolding the paper, she read, 'Kabeer will be followed and anyone who dares to come in between will be ruthlessly eliminated.'

She looked up from the paper, ashen. Somebody had been tailing them and probably knew exactly where they were. Kabeer was all alone in a strange city. She looked around, frantic with worry, but couldn't see him anywhere.

Kabeer kept walking along the dark streets of Multan in a dudgeon. He had fallen in love with Zoya almost instantly and in hindsight he suspected that the relationship and affection had been entirely one-sided. He had been just a convenient shoulder to cry on upon her bereavement and she had mistaken it for love.

It was growing late, but Kabeer was still walking off his rage and frustration, his hands deep in his pockets. He neither knew nor cared where he was headed. He turned into a street where there were no streetlights. It was only when he accidentally stepped on a pile of garbage that squished underfoot that he realized he was quite a distance from the beaten track. He took a step back, unsure if he still wanted to be alone.

From an alleyway at right angles to his street, a man clad in black emerged and began walking towards him. Kabeer decided to ask for directions and waited for the stranger to come closer. The man stopped in front of Kabeer. Although it was difficult to see his face in the dark, his intentions weren't. By the time Kabeer sensed danger and could react, it was too late. The man pulled out a hockey stick from the folds of his robes and dealt a heavy blow to Kabeer's head. Kabeer staggered sideways, but managed to stay upright. The man hit him again, this time on the back. Kabeer howled in agony. Out of nowhere, more people materialized from the shadows. Somebody covered his head with a black cloth. Kabeer struggled but was no match for the four burly men. A large hand covered his mouth and gagged him. Someone kicked him behind the knee and he buckled and fell to his knees. Another blow to the stomach and his head hit the ground. Kabeer couldn't move. He heard footsteps running away as his attackers left. He just lay there helplessly, hoping and praying that help would arrive. His head was bleeding and he was soaked in blood and ached all over. He tried to stay awake, but was dizzy with the pain and his eyes drooped shut . . .

Zoya was frantically driving through the lanes and bylanes, searching for Kabeer. She thought she heard a shriek over the roar of the car's engine. Hoping she hadn't imagined it, she turned into the street, her eyes peeled for any sign of Kabeer. A man in a black Pathani suit appeared out of nowhere and stood in front of the car, caught in her headlights. Her gut clenched in disgust as she recognized his face—her father.

His expression enigmatic as always, he turned into an alleyway and disappeared. Zoya parked and got out of the car. She saw a man lying unconscious on the ground, a few metres away. It was Kabeer.

She checked his pulse and was glad that he was still alive. She looked around the deserted street. Something clicked in her head about her father's inscrutable face.

CHAPTER 27

July '16

The doctors worked hard to restore Kabeer to some semblance of normalcy after the attack. Immediately upon receiving the news, Arko and the coach rushed to the hospital. Zoya was already there at Kabeer's bedside and remained in the hospital almost until midnight.

Arko was uncharacteristically quiet but his eyes reflected his worry. He thought it would be better if he spoke less and listened more, as Kabeer haltingly told them what had happened and reiterated that he didn't know who had felled him.

Zoya listened to the account, shocked and appalled. 'You were always bad with in-swingers, weren't you?' Arko gave a flickering smile and said.

'If I were as good as you, I would've left balls and players at the right time,' Kabeer winced as he tried to winked.

Thoughts jostled together in Zoya's head and she gave a perfunctory smile as Arko and Kabeer ribbed each other as was their wont. She was relieved that Kabeer was all right, but she was seriously considering bringing her father up on charges.

When the police arrived at the hospital, Kabeer and Arko brushed away the incident as an accident so it wouldn't be blown out of proportion into an act of terrorism and culminate in a war between the countries.

'We're sorry about the inconvenience, sir, but we have to go through the formalities and document your statement,' said the officer, his expression deadpan as he scribbled in his notebook.

'Sure,' Kabeer replied.

'Can you narrate the incident?'

Kabeer explained what had taken place—he had seen and heard nothing and didn't know who had hit him or why.

'So, you confirm that you were attacked with a hockey stick?'

'Is the weapon really important?' Arko asked acidly, 'shouldn't you be looking for the goons?'

'Sir, you might be a great cricketer but you are always bad with defence. To help you, our country has always been good at defence. So, please, let us do our work,' replied the policeman sternly.

'Thanks for letting us know, we've seen the finest of your defence displays in our last two tours,' replied Arko, who was in no mood to absorb insults.

'Sir, with all due respect, you're in Pakistan. So you have to abide by our systems. You've no other option.

'We'll make sure that the offender is found and punished, Mr Kabeer. We take great pride in our hospitality and this is definitely not our idea of hospitality. We look forward to seeing you back on the field soon,' said the policeman, completing his questionnaire and shaking hands with Kabeer.

As soon as they finished talking, Kabeer gestured to Arko that he needed to talk to Zoya in private. Arko, aware of the turn of events in the past few days, knew that they both needed time to sort things out.

The coach also left with Arko.

Zoya and Kabeer were alone now and the silence between them stretched taut.

When none of them said anything for the next few seconds, Kabeer picked up a magazine from his bedside table and started flipping through it. He cleared his throat a couple of times to get her attention. Then he kept the magazine back on the table and said, 'It's so lovely out here.'

'What?' Zoya raised her eyebrows.

'I was just starting a conversation,' Kabeer smiled tiredly and reached for her hand. 'Are you upset because of what happened or are you still mad at me?'

Zoya's smile was forced. Kabeer's eyes bore into hers and she tried maintaining eye contact, but every time she met his eyes, she was reminded of the fact that it was her own father who was gunning for Kabeer. She looked everywhere else except at him. She was terrified and her own breath drummed loudly in her ears. Zoya waited for a second before saying something that would change their lives forever.

'Leave Pakistan, Kabeer,' Zoya said softly, her eyes bright with tears, 'and as soon as possible.'

Everything grew still all at once.

'After the fiasco of this series, there's no question of my remaining in Pakistan.'

'I'm planning to book your flight to India tomorrow evening if the doctor discharges you,' Zoya looked into his eyes as she spoke. 'This country isn't safe for you any more.'

'As long as you're with me, it's going to be safe,' Kabeer smiled and squeezed her hand gently.

'I was with you all this while and there was nothing I could do to protect you,' Zoya replied.

Kabeer looked puzzled and shook his head.

'All I'm saying is, you don't belong here,' Zoya repeated firmly, 'You belong in India and that's where you should be.'

Kabeer paused for a few seconds, trying to comprehend what she meant. 'And what about us?'

'It would take us some time to pretend that we never existed for each other.'

'I wish it were as convenient as you make it out to be. I never thought that you would give up so easily,' Kabeer said softly. 'I was the one who was attacked today. But I've met people like you and Ghulam, who made me believe that our inherent cultures and people are the same despite the artificial barriers erected by superficial politics. I know it makes you uncomfortable, but I can't back down from this fight.'

'This isn't a great time to be talking about philosophy, Kabeer.'

'Let me finish, okay?' he said. 'That's precisely what your grandfather, Amaan Ali sahib, wanted.'

'I've lost enough people in my life, Kabeer, and I don't want to lose you as well.'

'Aren't you driving me away with this already?' Kabeer asked, tossing her hand away.

Arko knocked on the door and peeped in. 'Kabeer, Zoya. Sorry to intrude, but I think you need to hear this. The board has decided to abandon the rest of the tour and we're returning to India now,' Arko left shortly after dropping this bombshell.

'So this is really happening,' Kabeer thought.

They could feel themselves going away from each other as Zoya breathed heavily and said, 'I think it's best for everyone at the moment.'

She didn't want to cry in front of Kabeer, so she left the hospital. It was almost midnight as she drove to her hotel room in Multan.

Kabeer couldn't do anything but sit there, frozen, as he watched her leave. What had seemed like a dream to him, shattered in front of his eyes. He felt exhausted and drained after his physical and emotional ordeal. There were many questions lingering in his head, most important of all: 'Will we ever get to meet again?'

There was so much he wanted to tell her. He realized that in all this while that they had been together, he had never really opened up about his feelings for her, never told her how he fell in love with her. And all that had come to an end now, just like that. Poof! Gone.

CHAPTER 28

July '16

Zoya,

I never thought that I would write a love letter to you. It's always better to say these things in person, but circumstances never allowed us to do so.

The last few days have made me realize that the journey of life is erratic and changes its course whenever it pleases. I might have taken your name a little more than a thousand times in the last few days and I can't even begin to tell you what it does to me. However, taking your name today wasn't so easy because it reminded me of all our time spent together, which we may not get to relive after this day.

From the moment you left the hospital, you've been on my mind constantly.

I never told you but I liked you from the moment I saw your picture on a hoarding during my first visit to Pakistan and I always wished that I could tell you in person how astounded I was by your beauty. But in all honesty, you bowled me over when I actually saw you for real. You were more magnificent, standing before me, than any picture of yours I had ever seen. How optimum is the beauty that beats itself?

I was grateful to have met you during my first match in Pakistan. You swept me off my feet with your voice. For some weird reason, I felt a certain connection with you. After the gruesome attacks that day, I kept checking for updates on your recovery—on the news, Internet. I was elated a month after that when I found you were staying in the same hotel as me. Meeting you was nothing less than a dream coming true. After meeting you, I understood what it feels like to fall in love at first sight. Our first kiss will always remain special for me. It wasn't just a kiss, but with it, we became two bodies and one soul. And how can one bid goodbye to their own soul, Zoya?

No matter how much our countries hate each other, we belong together. I want you to be the first and last person in the crowd cheering for me in the stands and when you'll get old and wouldn't be able to walk, I will still be in the audience.

With this goodbye today, it'll be the first and probably the last time when I open my heart up to you. I might never be able to do it again in life, so I hope you understand my feelings more than the words.

We are yet to write a chapter of our lives together, so please don't close it midway. I have looked for you all my life and finally, when we were together, I find it hard to believe that you walked away. I've missed you more than I have ever missed anyone in my life and it's just going to get more difficult without you.

I want us to be the reason people believe in love over nationality and religion. Can you give us one more chance? Can you for once trust me. I can only hope to see you soon, this time in India.

Love,
Kabeer

CHAPTER 29

July '16

Later that evening, as the team landed in India, Arko pushed Kabeer on a wheelchair to collect their luggage from the carousel. They attracted curious stares from passers-by. Kabeer's broken legs were in plaster; he had been sewn and bandaged and still had purpling bruises on his face and neck.

Arko placed reassuring hands on Kabeer's shoulders as a swarm of reporters and cameramen flocked to see their returning heroes. On one of the airport's large television screens, Kabeer saw a news channel depicting image after image of him and Zoya together. A crowd was repeatedly chanting 'shame on Kabeer' as the police tried to hold them off.

Vishal Sharma was the journalist standing in front of the crowd, waving a placard with a #shameonkabeer poster. He rapidly spoke into the camera, pillorying Kabeer and inciting the crowd.

Kabeer thought he looked familiar and then he remembered. This was the same reporter who had questioned Zoya's priorities and suggested that her avarice trumped her affection for her grandfather.

'What have I done to receive so much of hatred from both countries?' Kabeer groaned.

* * *

As Kabeer struggled to shut the small, over-stuffed suitcase, his grandfather wandered in.

'I don't understand why you have to go back to that wretched country where you almost died,' the old man grumbled. 'What if something terrible happens again?'

'Then the family gets a compensation,' Kabeer grinned and wrapped his arms around him.

'How many times do I have to tell you not to joke about these things?' his mother scolded.

'I told you to not let him play cricket. If he had cleared his CAT exams, he would've been working for a multi-national company,' his grandfather snapped, stepping away from Kabeer.

'I travel abroad regularly and earn a lot more than those boardroom giants, so what's the problem?'

'They aren't putting their lives at risk.'

'What's your problem with Pakistan, Dadu? I've grown up listening to your hate stories about Pakistanis but when I went there, all I got was love.'

'So, those bullets that the terrorists used to kill people had love written on them? I don't care how you're going to do it, but you're taking your name off that list.'

'As vice-captain, Dadu, I can't do that.'

'The players who took their names off the list weren't fools.'

'Maybe they were, maybe they weren't,' Kabeer snapped the recalcitrant suitcase shut, 'but it's time for me to demonstrate my sportsmanship both on and off the field. Please let me go now,' Kabeer said, as he touched his grandfather's feet before leaving the house for the tour.

It was a distressed household that Kabeer left behind. His father and grandfather were cross as crabs and his mother wept. His grandfather, who had been born in Pakistan himself, was very anti-Pakistan now with reports of rampant terrorism and violence in that country. Furthermore, they all felt it was dangerous for Kabeer to visit Pakistan in the current climate, especially as he had been targeted by violent elements there.

As he was leaving the house, his Dadu shouted, 'When something bad happens, he'll remember me.'

'Don't say that, Papa. He's your grandson,' Kabeer's mother cried.

'Then why doesn't he listen to me! It's a dangerous state and the people there are even more treacherous.'

'You too were born in Pakistan, Papa.'

'It was India back then. Pakistan is this new and strange country that sponsors terrorism, hate and deaths.'

'There are people out there who are just like us.'

'Those people can't be like us. Mark my words. They are Pakistanis and they'll remain the same. Do not even compare them with Indians,' his grandfather scoffed, and walked away in anger. He was aware of the risks involved, but he also knew that his grandson wouldn't listen to him. Every time anyone visited Pakistan, only one question lingered in his mind, 'Will he ever come back?'

There were many things he wanted to tell Kabeer. Things that had remained unsaid for years. As he lay on the couch, he thought, 'Kabeer has only seen my hate for Pakistan but he still doesn't know the reason behind it.'

CHAPTER 30

July '16

Lahore was being lashed by a tropical hurricane. Despite securing the doors and windows, Zoya could hear the gale, whooshing and whistling around the house as if it were trying to break in. She stood by the window, watching the gigantic trees in the backyard bend and sway at the whim of the wind. To Zoya, the weather conditions were far tamer than the storm within her. Her future with Kabeer was shrouded in a grey fog.

She heard the bell ring and her stomach clenched. She knew it wasn't going to be a pleasant conversation even before she unlocked the door.

Her father stood on the stoop, drenched to the skin in the short dash from his car to the house.

'How about a towel?' he asked.

She noticed that he was in the same black Pathani suit that he had worn on the night that Kabeer had been attacked. Zoya handed him a large turkey towel and was taken aback to see that he was wearing plastic gloves.

'Were you on a murder spree?'

'What kind of a question is that?' Danish laughed it off.

'Why the gloves?'

'I have an allergy to certain fabrics, so I use the 'murder gloves'. You and I have never actually spent time together so you're naturally unaware of my condition,' he sat down on the couch. 'So, what did you want to talk to me about?' Danish smiled.

'Nothing really. It's been a while since we chatted so I invited you over.'

'Of all the days you chose today when I had to battle the deluge, the traffic and the fallen trees,' he chuckled. 'I guess parents don't have too much choice, do they?'

'But whether the child wants it or not, the parent could choose to provide her with a stepmother.'

'I married another woman so I could protect you and you walked off.'

'Protect me? You hit mum on a regular basis and that is all I remember of you during my childhood.'

162

'Which is why I wanted to do everything right the second time around, but you never gave me a second chance.'

'You were busy exploring the space between the legs of that bitch you call your second wife!' Zoya sneered. Danish reached over and backhanded her. Zoya fell on the carpeted floor. 'Why don't you accept that you were just being a lusty cock by marrying her?' she scoffed.

'Watch your mouth,' Danish growled.

'Otherwise, you'll murder me like you tried murdering Kabeer?'

'Now, you're talking rubbish,' Danish dismissed his daughter's accusations.

'I was there when you hit him and made your escape.'

'What proof do you have? Show your proof to the person who tried to leak intimate pictures of you with Kabeer.'

'What do you mean?'

Danish sighed and raised his hands in a gesture that said, God, give me strength. 'You know, for more than a decade now I've wondered what would happen if I admitted to you that I was wrong to treat your mother the way I did. You don't have a forgiving bone in your body. But I was always there, supporting you from behind the scenes—when your visa needed to get cleared, when your Mamu jaan tried taking advantage of your situation, and whenever you needed any kind of help. You just never noticed that I was silently playing my role as a father.'

He stood up, walked over to the window and stared out at the storm, 'I was playing the role of your guardian angel and tailing Kabeer to figure out whether he was right for you. I discovered an ugly truth when you saw me that night as Kabeer lay unconscious.'

Zoya stood up now, her eyes unblinking as she gazed at Danish's reflection in the windowpane, a reflection that was distorted by the rain flowing down the other side of the glass.

'He was beaten mercilessly that day by one of your relatives. Your Mamu jaan.'

Zoya couldn't believe her ears. Would Mamu jaan stoop so low? But why?

Danish took out a photograph of her Mamu jaan, dressed in black, along with a bunch of his goons, beating up Kabeer. 'I was in the shadows, watching when this was taking place. Your uncle saw my camera flash and immediately ran away from the scene along with the rest of his henchmen.'

'Why click a picture instead of saving Kabeer?' Zoya was incredulous.

'I didn't want to get into any trouble just before the elections,' he said, shaking his head. 'Also, if those thugs had turned on me and I had lost my life in an attempt to save his, there would have been no one left to tell you what I'm telling you today.'

It was at that juncture that Zoya resolved to go to India to see Kabeer.

CHAPTER 31

October '16

It had been a couple of tough months for Kabeer both physically and mentally as there was radio silence from Zoya. It wasn't like he tried contacting her either, but deep down he had hoped that Zoya would be the one to contact him first to enquire about his health, respond to his letter or send a word of acknowledgement at the very least.

Kabeer wished they had spent more time together before rushing headlong into a relationship. It would have given them a chance to get to know each other better.

Kabeer made an amazing recovery, zipped through his medical tests and was back on his feet a couple of months later. He returned to the nets for a rigorous practice session on his birthday.

He felt elated as he walked into the field and was welcomed with open arms by his team members.

At the end of a very long and exhausting day at the nets, Arko, Rehaan, Rishabh, Shaurya and the other teammates who had smuggled in two drummers into the grounds, hoisted Kabeer on their shoulders and carried him in a victory march around of the field.

After a crazy celebration at a local pub, everybody decided to call it a day and returned to their hotel.

Kabeer wandered back into the grounds where practice was still going on. He hadn't realized just how much he had missed all this.

The coach, who had remained at the nets to compile his notes for strategies, came over to Kabeer, 'Aren't you going back home for more celebrations, Kabeer?'

'Not yet, sir. I need to get in a lot more practice before the domestic season begins.'

'You can do that tomorrow.'

'Just a couple more hours and then I'll go home to celebrate with my family.'

'Okay. Knock yourself out,' the coach grinned.

He spent the next couple of minutes thinking about Zoya. *It might have been nice of her to at least remember my birthday, it hasn't been that long since I had mentioned it*, he thought. All this while that they'd stayed apart, he had wished his birthday would be a time when he would definitely get a call from her. With the day about to come to an end, and still no greeting from her, he felt that the last thread that had tied them together, had also snapped.

He had always been more of a batsman than a bowler. He decided to exercise his bowling arm and made several fast deliveries at the stumps with the speedometer monitoring his speed. Because bowling wasn't his forte, he had to stay very focused on his practice. This concentration prevented him from brooding about Zoya. The speedometer registered 132 kilometres per hour and then 137 and suddenly rose to 141 kilometres per hour on his third delivery. He was jubilant.

At that moment he heard a familiar sound, the special ringtone he had set for Zoya. He was beaming from ear to ear as he answered the call.

'Kabeer.'

'Zoya.'

'How are you?'

'Very impatient and a little hopeful.'

'Hopeful for?'

'Hopeful that I would get to talk to you.'

'And impatient?'

'Because my hopes were really testing my patience.'

'Why didn't you call?'

'I was hoping that you would call me.'

'Why?'

'Because I wanted some answers.'

'And the questions to which were?'

'Many. Did I really mean something to you or was I merely in the right place at the right time and now you've gotten over me?'

'Did I say that?'

'You certainly acted like I was a phase.'

There was a pregnant silence for several minutes. Kabeer was aware that his words had stung.

'Oh. Thank you for letting me know, Kabeer,' Zoya said finally.

'I didn't mean it that way, Zoya—' he trailed off, realizing he had put his foot in his mouth.

After another short silence, Zoya laughed merrily. Kabeer stood speechless, as Zoya kept giggling and then laughed harder. Her laughter was infectious and music to his ears. He couldn't stop himself and unwillingly joined her, their laughter echoing in the night.

'You're just beyond ridiculous.' Kabeer said, a little subdued.

'I have already put you through the wringer. I promise I won't torture you any more.'

'I wouldn't snatch that credit from you.'

'I've come to Mumbai today to celebrate your birthday. Happy birthday, Kabeer. I'll be outside the stadium if you've got a few minutes to meet a girl who has come all the way to Mumbai from Pakistan just for you. Also, I've booked a cab, which is here already.'

'You've got to be kidding!' Kabeer abruptly disconnected the call and ran to the gate. There were cars zipping past under the streetlights, but no sign of Zoya or anybody else. There was no cab waiting. He was clueless. Where was she?

This was the worst kind of joke that she could have played on him. It didn't seem like Zoya at all.

All of a sudden, a hand covered his eyes from behind. Kabeer froze, inhaling the perfume that wafted off the love of his life. Ever so gently he covered her soft hand and drew it away from his face. His eyes met hers and time seemed to stand still.

Her cheeks were pink with excitement and she looked even more ravishing than ever. Kabeer was the happiest man in the world to have her standing in front of him after what seemed like ages. She was in a black crop top and a blue tartan mini skirt combined with knee-high socks and pencil-heeled boots. Her arched eyebrows defined her mesmerizing eyes. Kabeer skipped a heartbeat as she curled her lips into a beautiful smile and winked at him.

Silently, she pointed her finger to something behind Kabeer and he turned around to find balloons and candle-lit lanterns rise up into the sky from all directions. There were red ones, yellow ones, white ones, heart-shaped ones, and smiley ones. Soon enough, dozens of them were up in the sky, when the last and the biggest one followed, reaching high up, with 'Happy Birthday' written across it. The sky looked like a magical garden of balloons proclaiming his happiness to the world at large.

Kabeer was speechless.

'Say something,' Zoya whispered.

He slowly looked down at Zoya, 'There are no words to express myself at this moment. I mean, thank you. Nobody has ever done anything like this for me. I've never done anything like this for anyone. How could you even plan something on this scale in a whole other country? I'm overwhelmed. Thank you,' he hugged her.

'I have my methods, my dear,' she said archly, and then blushed rosily.

'And to see you here, Zoya, thank you so much for coming all the way,' Kabeer said gathering both her hands into his.

'You needn't articulate your emotions all the time, your eyes say it all. Your letter did half the job, I must admit. You're an excellent writer.' A stretch limousine drew up and a chauffeur in white regalia emerged. He held the door open for them and waited.

'Now, this is something unexpected. Where are we going?'

'I have it all planned out and want you to willingly surrender yourself to me,' she whispered into his ear.

'Do with me as you will,' he smiled and gallantly helped her into the car and followed her in.

They caught up with all the news of the incidents and events that had taken place during the time that they had been apart as the car drove around the city. The chauffeur pulled over in front of the grand five-star hotel near Bandstand. This was where Zoya was staying. The chauffeur opened the door for them and Zoya held Kabeer's hand and drew him through the main door and to the elevator. She placed a finger on his lips as they ascended to the roof.

It was the most glorious view of Mumbai he had ever seen. He stood looking down at the city spread below, far and wide. Living in Mumbai for so many years, he had never imagined the city to be so beautiful. He didn't even realize that he had been holding his breath until Zoya came from behind him and put her hand on his shoulder.

He appreciated that Zoya had gone so far out of her way to make this surprise happen.

The dining table in the middle of the roof garden restaurant was beautifully laid out with a white lace tablecloth and placemats. A magnificent birthday cake stood in the centre surmounted with one lighted candle. Kabeer felt deeply embarrassed as he cut the cake and the hotel staff sang 'Happy Birthday'. Zoya laughed as he fed her a slice and she immediately reciprocated with an even bigger slice.

'You've made me feel so special, Zoya. I can't thank you enough. You made my day. In the last couple of months, I thought I would lose you, but thanks for everything.'

'Anything for you, Kabeer. You have made me feel like no one ever has. I adore you and everything about you. The least I could do is make you happy on your happiest day,' she said, taking his cold palm in hers and warming it.

The staff dispersed and they sat down to wait for their candlelight dinner. Kabeer reached for her hand, 'Your presence made my day all the more special. There's nothing more that I could have asked for on my birthday,' he said. Zoya couldn't help but grin from ear to ear. Kabeer just wanted to jump off the table and kiss those beautiful pink lips and never let go for a long time. He couldn't believe that someone so smart, funny and perfect in every way would go out of her way and do so much for him.

'What are you thinking about?'

'I was thinking about how much I truly enjoyed planning this evening. It has been my pet project over the last few months,' she laughed.

'And I'll cherish this memory forever, thank you so much, my dear.'

For a long time, neither of them spoke and sat in companionable silence. The food arrived along with a bottle of red wine. Their dinner conversation was desultory and easy as they enjoyed the past.

During the post-dinner promenade in the well-appointed gardens of the establishment, Zoya stopped and said, 'Would you excuse me for a moment? I just need to collect something from my room. I'll be back in a jiffy.'

Kabeer sat down on a bench by a fountain. The entire evening felt unreal and he was worried that he would wake up and find it was all just a dream.

Could he actually get married to her someday? He knew that because he was an Indian and she was a Pakistani could cause trouble for them, but somehow he felt he could take on any troubles that came his way, as long as he was with her.

Zoya returned with a gift-wrapped package.

Kabeer shook his head, 'What's in it, Zoya?'

'Find out for yourself,' she replied with a mysterious smile and walked away.

Kabeer opened the wrapping paper to reveal a Walkman with a cassette inside. There was a note stuck inside with the words, 'Play the audio cassette.'

'Oh, the old way.'

'Because classic will always remain the best.'

He chuckled as he plugged in the earphones and pressed 'play'.

Zoya's voice came through the player:

'Hi, Kabeer, if you're listening to this, it means I've successfully carried out my plans for this evening. I hope you've enjoyed it so far. I sincerely hope you like this last surprise. I've not had a chance to speak with you during the last two months and I missed you so very much. I've decided to record this audio to tell you about certain things.

'Before I met you, I had started to lose my faith in love. But you made me feel so loved from the moment I first saw you. I don't know what I thought, but for some reason, I wanted to keep talking to you. Our first kiss wasn't planned and we hadn't even started dating by then but I think that's what is special about both of us. We follow our heart more than our minds.

'You brought me love and peace, there's nothing more that I could've asked God to give me. I am able to open up my heart to you without hesitation, express my emotions without the fear of being judged. You can be the sincerest and the stupidest person at the same time. You understand me every day, every hour, every moment. Love seems more real and makes more sense than I thought it ever would.

'I know we'll have our fair share of fights like everybody else and sometimes, we'll feel like we can't take it any more. I know we belong to two different countries that are bound to hate each other but I am also sure that we'll be able to overcome our differences and come out stronger. Nobody in the world can complete me the way you do.

'I have waited for a special occasion to tell you this, and I guess, there's no better occasion than today, your birthday. I propose to love you forever and remain by your side during both the good and the bad.

'Would you like to make me a small yet important part of your life, Kabeer? I am waiting for you just a few metres away. Kiss me if you love me, and turn away if you don't. I love you.'

Kabeer was moved by what he heard. He kept the Walkman aside and started walking towards Zoya. She was trying to merge with the shadows, but a smile flickered on her face as Kabeer reached her. He gently cupped her cheeks and they kissed deeply. Kabeer breathed, 'I love you, Zoya. This has been the best evening of my life and I can't wait to spend the rest of my life with you.'

Zoya replied softly, 'I love you too, Kabeer. I am yours, always.' She finally handed over one last note that said: 'To spend this journey called life with you, I've decided to come a little closer to you; I've come to Mumbai, finally and forever. I am going to give our love a second chance if you're willing to. I am going to stay in your country if it treats me as one of you. I am going to be an Indian, who would still be a Pakistani at heart, if you're ready to be a Pakistani who would be an Indian at heart for me.'

'Happy birthday, Kabeer,' she whispered. 'This is the best gift I could ever get!' Kabeer replied and hugged her.

CHAPTER 32

October '16

Kabeer and Zoya were nesting and looking for an apartment in Mumbai. They took time out of their busy schedules to meet for lunches, dinners or to just grab a cup of coffee and compared notes to see how their apartment hunt was panning out.

'Lokhandwala, Versova and Veera Desai flats rejected me for being a Pakistani,' she wrote down in her little logbook.

'Where are we heading today?' Zoya was at the dressing table, about to apply her make-up.

'Will your make-up match the locality?' Kabeer raised himself on his elbow to watch her.

'I certainly don't want ugliness to be the reason for rejection.'

'That's so not going to happen,' Kabeer swung his long legs out of the bed and rose in magnificent nakedness.

Zoya warded him off, 'Not until I get an apartment for us.'

They reached their destination and Kabeer parked the car as he saw the broker waiting for them.

'Hello,' Kabeer greeted Ajay Apte from Happy Real Estate. The broker ignored Kabeer and beamed at Zoya, who looked lovely in her crop top, skinny jeans and sunglasses.

He looked at her up and down gravely and said, 'You should've worn salwar kameez.'

'Why?' Zoya asked in confusion.

'*Hindustani ladkiyon pe yeh chote kapde shobha nahi dete*, madam,' Apte replied.

'*Par main* Pakistani *hoon.*'

'Hindustan–Pakistan are brother and sister, madam,' said Apte patronizingly. Zoya frowned.

A security man stopped the trio at the gates of the gated community, insisting they sign the guest entry register.

'Don't you know these two?' Apte asked the man.

'Still need the signature,' he said resolutely. Kabeer quickly registered on behalf of everyone, not wanting to make a national incident about it.

The owner of the apartment, a tall, bald, middle-aged man, graciously invited them in.

'You need not take off your shoes. It's fine,' Apte told Zoya and Kabeer.

'No, it is not,' the owner said, frowning at Apte. Zoya and Kabeer dutifully removed their shoes at the entrance. After taking an entire tour of the apartment, Zoya looked really happy.

They returned to the living room to close the deal. The owner sat across from them on one of the sofas and started typing furiously on his phone. He didn't pay any attention to the potential tenants. Meanwhile, Zoya, Kabeer and Apte waited awkwardly. Finally, the broker cleared his throat and said, 'Sir, Zoya madam wants to rent this apartment.'

'Zoya?'

'Yes.'

'You're Muslim?' He turned to look at her.

It was clear that the landlord wasn't aware of Kabeer and Zoya's celebrity statuses and when Zoya was introduced, he scowled at Apte, 'Yes.'

'This is a gated community purely for Hindus, so Muslims are unacceptable.'

'Sir, she is a good woman. She won't create any trouble. Just tell her the rent.'

'The housing society won't allow her to stay here, Apte,' his tone was softer this time, as he shook his head and smiled apologetically.

'The secretary is a good friend, so this won't be an issue,' replied Apte.

'Oh, all right then, it'll be an eleven-month lease agreement. No drinks. No boys. No late-night parties,' the owner reeled off the list by rote.

'What's the rent?' Zoya asked.

'Rs 50,000 rent plus Rs 2 lakh deposit.'

'Done.' Zoya accepted the terms and conditions without batting an eyelid. Kabeer raised his eyebrows at her.

'What do you do?' the owner asked her.

'I am a singer,' Zoya replied. He gave her a look and said, 'Nice. Nowadays kids are delving into creative fields. My son too wanted to be a singer but he doesn't have a good voice, so we made sure he realized that.'

Zoya didn't respond.

'I'll need Xerox copies of your Aadhaar card and PAN card for finalizing the agreement.'

'I don't have an Aadhaar card or PAN card,' Zoya said hesitantly, as Kabeer and Apte looked at each other, tensed that this might be the point where they lost the apartment.

'Why?'

'Because I am not an Indian, I am a Pakistani,' Zoya replied, in a low voice. The owner laughed it off. 'You're a Pakistani. Where is your gun?' He laughed harder. Zoya looked offended but didn't say anything.

'I am a Pakistani and we travel without guns, just like you Indians,' she replied firmly.

The owner looked at her and then at Kabeer in confusion. He finally turned to Apte. 'What were you thinking bringing a Pakistani to my home, Apte?'

'Why are you making a big deal out of it? She'll be no trouble.'

But the apartment owner flew up into the boughs about it and threatened to call the police. Kabeer stepped in at this juncture and told the furious landlord to back off. 'You're crossing your limits, sir.'

'If I cross my limits, all of you will be in trouble. It's better that y'all leave. This is my flat and I won't have a tenant who comes from a nation that sponsors terrorism and kills my countrymen.'

'I can say the same thing about your nation as well, sir,' Zoya replied furiously.

'Shut up! Can you please shut up?' Kabeer told her exasperatedly as she looked at him in shock.

Zoya flounced out of the apartment; Kabeer followed. They didn't say a word until they were back in the car and heading back to the hotel.

'He was insulting my nation and you asked me to shut up?'

'No-no. See, he was getting hyper and I didn't want you to get into any trouble. If he would have called the police, you would've landed yourself in a fine mess, baby.' Kabeer held her hands and kissed her forehead. 'Don't worry. You're my responsibility. I'll find you a nice apartment. I promise,' he smiled.

It was getting dark and the roads were fairly empty. 'I want to drive,' said Zoya.

'It's Mumbai,' protested Kabeer. 'These roads aren't really safe.'

'They're no different from the streets back home. Please, Kabeer?'

'I can never refuse you anything,' Kabeer gave in.

'Thanks for having my back today,' said Zoya after they swapped places in the car.

'I should've slapped that dog for insulting your country.'

'We're used to it,' shrugged Zoya. 'What matters is the opinion of one's close ones. I loved the India of my grandfather's anecdotes. I truly want to be loved that way someday.'

'You'll receive adulation beyond your expectations, Zoya. People in my country are known for their warmth and hospitality.'

Zoya smiled and said nothing.

'What?'

'I don't want to be the favourite guest, Kabeer. I want to be a part of you all. What I seek with you is permanence.'

A traffic police vehicle flagged down their car at that moment. She drew up at the kerb and rolled down her window.

A policeman got out of the jeep and approached the window on the driver's side, 'Your licence, please.'

Zoya handed over her driver's licence.

The cop looked shocked, 'It's a Pakistani licence.'

'I am a Pakistani, sir,' Zoya replied. He withdrew and rapidly spoke into his walkie-talkie before coming back to the car. 'Show me your passport.'

'It's in my hotel room.'

'Is there a problem, officer?' Kabeer leaned across Zoya.

'That's unacceptable, ma'am,' said the policeman, ignoring Kabeer, 'I am afraid you'll have to accompany me to the police station.' He signalled to the police jeep parked on the side of the road. Zoya was made to get into the jeep. She felt humiliated sitting in the squad vehicle with the uniformed policemen.

'I am with you, Zoya, don't worry. Everything will be all right,' Kabeer said reassuringly as the jeep set off.

He followed the jeep in the car. For the first time in weeks, Zoya realized how much she missed her own country.

Another car pulled up alongside, parallel to the jeep. Zoya saw someone holding a large camera and a flash went off as the person clicked her picture. She recognized the face. *Vishal Sharma.*

CHAPTER 33

October '16

Zoya knew the police. She had grown up in Pakistan amongst politicians and police personnel and knew that when the police decided that you were the enemy it was nigh impossible to win them over. In Pakistan, however, she wasn't afraid of the long arm of the law because her father was a politician and her grandfather, a celebrity.

Although she wasn't entirely taken by surprise, she wasn't prepared for this situation just as yet. A police officer went through the routine formalities and noted down her details.

'Zoya Malik?' the police officer said, squinting at her driving licence.

'Yes, sir.'

'Pakistani?' the inspector asked.

'Yes, sir,' Zoya replied and looked into his eyes.

'Sir, can we drop this, please?' said Kabeer.

'Oh, are you Zoya?' a policeman asked.

'No, sir,' Kabeer said, quietly.

'Do not interfere in matters of the nation, Mr Kabeer. She's a Pakistani.'

'So? She's a human being, like an Indian.'

'Sarabjit was human too. Did you see what happened to him?' he snapped. 'Where's your passport?' the officer turned to Zoya.

'In my hotel.'

'What's it doing there? Planting a bomb?' he asked.

'If any one of you could accompany me, I'll be happy to show you my passport.'

'We're not your travel agents, miss,' interjected a constable.

'But if it's a concern of national security—,' Zoya replied politely.

'Rao, you'll go to the hotel and check the necessary documents, visa and passport,' the inspector said. 'And madam, we're letting you go this time, but in the future, try and respect the rules of the country you're in.

Zoya was ordered to get into the jeep and as before, Kabeer followed her in his car to the hotel. He could see the hurt and humiliation in her eyes. This wasn't the love he promised and he thumped the steering wheel in frustration. As the jeep sped up after the signal turned green, he noticed a media van following them and someone with a camera held to his face was leaning out, clicking as many pictures as he could. He recognized the man immediately.

When he saw Zoya in tears, Kabeer swerved and positioned his car between the police jeep and the media vehicle. To avoid a collision with an oncoming van, Sharma's van braked sharply. Kabeer and the police jeep crossed the next signal while it was still green, but the light had turned red by the time Sharma arrived at the junction. Kabeer and Zoya managed to get to the hotel in record time and complete the passport verification.

'Please carry your passport always,' Rao said as Kabeer quietly palmed into the cop's greasy fist 500-rupee note.

As soon as Rao left, Zoya crumpled down to the floor, sobbing. Kabeer ran towards her and hugged her.

'I don't understand what's happening, Kabeer!' she wept.

'I don't either,' he replied.

'My Naanu jaan always told me that it's politics that is ruining the relationships between our countries,' said Zoya bitterly, 'but that the people still love each other. I'm not sure that holds true any more.'

'That's not true, Zoya.'

'See what happened to you in Pakistan and what's happening to me in India.'

'Zoya, there are good and kind people here and in Pakistan, but there are bad elements in both countries as well. That shouldn't change our perception.

'I have been insulted for being a Pakistani. How do you expect me to not change my perception?'

'I've almost been murdered twice in Pakistan and that didn't change my faith in humanity, be it in Pakistan or elsewhere,' Kabeer replied, putting his arms around her.

'Do you know why I never gave up in Pakistan? Because I knew you'd be there for me no matter what happened and you wouldn't let anything bad happen to me. You were my biggest support there and I want to be your biggest support here.' Kabeer said, as he wiped her tears. 'No matter what happens, I will be by your side, always. I wouldn't let this hate impinge upon our love. We love each other for a reason. Don't forget that we decided to be the reason people believe in love.'

Zoya smiled through her tears.

'We take bullets for each other and that's the way we are, OK?' Kabeer remarked as he kissed her forehead. 'We have come incredibly far in our relationship and we face fear and all the good times together from here. Do you understand me?' Zoya nodded.

'Also, I've punctured the tyre of the police jeep,' Kabeer grinned.

Zoya laughed and lifted her face to kiss him. The tension melted, to be replaced by passion.

Later, as they lay intertwined in each other's arms that night, she asked, 'What happened to our flat-hunting?'

'You live with me. Now and forever,' Kabeer replied.

CHAPTER 34

October '16

They decided that Zoya would shift to his Mumbai apartment the very next day.

After checking out, they walked down to the hotel's parking lot where Kabeer had parked his car the previous evening. A shocking sight met their eyes, his car window had been smashed. Kabeer opened the door to reveal shards of glass on the driver's seat. He cleared it away silently and wrapped up the glass in the orange dusting cloth from the glove compartment. Zoya helped him. Wordlessly, he placed Zoya's luggage in the boot and they drove away.

Although Zoya didn't say anything, her silence spoke volumes. During the journey, Zoya thought of all the possible outcomes of her decision to remain in India. It would impact her career greatly. She didn't want to admit her misgivings to Kabeer.

'Surprise.' Everyone yelled, jumping out of their hiding places when Kabeer entered his home, but were taken aback on seeing Zoya. His family had been waiting eagerly for him, but were confused when they saw that he had brought Zoya along.

Karan broke the ice, 'Can I have your autograph, please?' he asked excitedly and insisted on clicking a selfie with her.

'Offer them greetings,' Kabeer whispered into Zoya's ears.

'What's—?' Zoya was about to blurt out in her nervousness but Kabeer immediately stopped her.

'They're my parents. Not your friends.'

'As-Salamu-Alaykum,' Zoya smiled at Kabeer's parents.

'Jai Shri Krishna,' replied Kabeer's mother, her palms together in greeting.

'This is Zoya Malik, right?' she asked her younger son, who gave an affirmative nod.

'My birthday was several days ago,' Kabeer said, 'so what's with the celebration?'

'It's our anniversary today, Kabeer, how could you forget?' his father chided him. Kabeer touched his parents' feet as was his customary greeting.

'Ooops, I forgot. I am so sorry.'

His grandfather walked in looked grumpy and then stopped dead upon seeing Zoya.

'We need to talk,' he growled at Kabeer and walked away. Kabeer's mother was not happy about this situation either, but she did her best to make Zoya feel welcome in their home.

Zoya was delighted with the guest bedroom that had been allocated to her. She was aware that there were undercurrents about her presence here with Kabeer and hoped with all her heart that time, the great healer, would eventually sort things out.

'Beta, what's going on with you two?' Kabeer's mother whispered as Zoya put her luggage aside.

'They're dating, Ma. It's all over the news,' Karan said with a smile on his face. He was the only one who looked happy.

'Shut up! Kabeer, tell me?'

'No, Ma. It' nothing like that.' The moment Kabeer said it, Zoya glared at him.

'I mean, she loves me,' Kabeer blurted. His mother gasped in shock.

'And I love her too,' Kabeer said. His mother started tearing up.

'I am going back home. My son loves a Pakistani girl. I can't live any more!' she wailed and rushed inside.

'At least listen to him once,' Kabeer's father called out to her as he went inside to calm his wife down.

'Mom is just a little shocked but she'll come around, don't worry,' said Karan, bustling in with her suitcases. 'Do you have a sister or friend as beautiful as you?' he asked.

Zoya couldn't help laughing.

Kabeer went inside to placate his mother. 'Why can't you be nice to the person who has just met you? Why do you have to judge her based on where she is from?'

'Why can't you be nice to the person who has given birth to you, without judging her for judging a Pakistani?'

'Because that's not what I've been taught by you. You always taught me to love people, and I love her.' At this, his mother started crying even more hysterically. Kabeer exchanged a look with his father. They knew what she was doing. Whenever something did not go according to her, she would start crying and pretending to lose her breath. She had always been good at it.

'You couldn't find anyone else to fall in love with?' she screamed.

'When he has already decided what's good for him, who are we to interfere?' his grandfather walked into the room and said. 'There's always a catch with you, isn't there? You do make the most unexpected decisions and don't even include us in them.'

'She isn't one of us, beta,' said his mother. 'I've heard of Pakistani girls luring Indian men to their doom.'

'Ma, I assure you, she has no such hidden agenda.'

'What do you even know about her?'

'She's the granddaughter of Amaan Ali Malik, the maestro, who loved India unconditionally even after the Partition,' Kabeer said.

'It's can't be that simple,' said his mother who was feeling distraught.

'It isn't complicated, mom,' replied Kabeer. 'Believe me, I understand how you feel, but she protected me in her own country and she's the reason I'm alive today. She makes me feel loved and wanted and no matter how hard I try, I'll never be able to do what she did for me in Pakistan.'

'We have to answer to this society, beta. They will never accept this union.'

'You can either worry about their judgement or be happy that your son found love in a beautiful soul who left everything in Pakistan to be with him,' Kabeer argued.

Zoya entered the room at that moment and looked timidly around at the stormy countenances in the room. She held the door open and the maid came in trundling the tea trolley.

'I've heard that tea helps when people feel stressed out, so I fixed us all a pot of tea,' Zoya smiled. Kabeer's father gallantly stepped forward, led Zoya to the couch and gestured to the maid to wheel in the trolley to the table at the centre of the room. Zoya gracefully poured out the tea into the dainty cups she had found in the kitchen cupboard. Although Kabeer's mother still looked mutinous, she was slightly mollified by Zoya's peace offering. She put two spoons of sugar in every cup, except in Kabeer's father's one.

'You won't put sugar in my cup?' his father asked.

'No, you have sugar. I already put sugar-free in your tea,' and with that everyone smiled, except for Kabeer's mother.

Kabeer's grandfather too continued to scowl ferociously and after a few minutes stormed out in a rage. Everybody went quiet in the room. Zoya bit her lip.

The sound of glass shattering broke the lull and was immediately followed by the old man's howl of pain. Everybody ran towards the noise that had come from the conservatory behind the house and found Kabeer's grandfather lying face down amidst shards of glass. His head was bleeding where the rock had struck him. The rock had smashed through the glass pane of the roof of the conservatory.

CHAPTER 35

October '16

They were at the hospital, outside the observation ward, tensely awaiting the doctor's verdict.

Zoya softly touched Kabeer's arm. 'Are we ever going to overcome all this, Kabeer?' she asked.

His mother was standing at a distance, studiously ignoring both Kabeer and Zoya.

'We're fine, Zoya,' he said softly, 'these adversities will only make us stronger.' He led Zoya to his mother and put an arm around each of them. His mother was stiff and resistant.

'He'll be fine, Ma' said Kabeer, and the older woman bent her head and wiped her eyes with the edge of her sari. Kabeer's father came over and hugged her comfortingly. He looked over his wife's head and saw Zoya's worried face. He gave her an encouraging smile.

A doctor emerged from the observation room. 'There's nothing to worry about,' he said. 'He's fine. There has been some blood loss, but he's good. I've given him something so he's sleeping now. You can take him home in a day or two and we'll send someone over to remove the sutures.'

Kabeer's grandfather seemed to have undergone a change of heart during his incarceration at the hospital because when he regained consciousness, the old man hugged Zoya apologizing to her for behaving like a bear with a sore head.

Two days later, Kabeer's grandfather received a hero's welcome upon his return home.

Kabeer's mother also seemed to have reconciled to the idea of a Muslim daughter-in-law. For the first time, Zoya spent quality time with Kabeer's family.

Unfortunately, their persecution persisted unabated. Although some political leaders released statements time and again in attempts to harass Kabeer and Zoya, the extra police protection ensured that they weren't physically harmed.

Kabeer's family was targeted and heckled by their neighbours and acquaintances and Karan was bullied by some unsavoury elements in his college. However, the family as a whole valiantly weathered these storms.

Zoya was surprised and delighted with the love and acceptance that she received from Kabeer's family and she stayed with them for a whole month; a month that filled her with a sense of belonging. When his family returned to Pune, they bid her a fond farewell and apologized for any hurt or pain they may have inadvertently caused her.

Later that night, as Zoya packed her bags for another hectic tour, Kabeer asked petulantly, 'Why do you have to stay in a hotel when your concert is in Mumbai?'

'It's not just getting back to work, I also need to get used to staying in hotels for days on end. Furthermore, when the sponsors are sparing no expense on these stays, why shouldn't I let them pamper me?'

'At the cost of staying away from me?' Kabeer asked.

Zoya smiled at him and unzipped one of the bags. He was delighted to see his clothes in it, tidily folded and stacked.

Zoya teased him, 'You have no choice, Mr Kabeer, but to accompany me for the entire tour. You have a month off from the nets and I couldn't think of a better idea than this.'

Kabeer kissed her lingeringly and whispered, 'I love you.' Zoya giggled as he kissed every inch of her and punctuated each kiss with a fervent 'I love you'.

Moments where everything is beautiful and real, every kiss has its own meaning. Sometimes it takes us into a different world and sometimes it makes our existing world full of beauty.

Zoya kissed him back, 'I can't live without you, Kabeer.'

CHAPTER 36

October '16

There's a special place in this world where nobody is judged for who they are. They are simply allowed to live and grow. That place is called love.

Kabeer and Zoya were on an endless quest for this place both in Pakistan and in India. After a two-hour-long flight, following a hugely successful concert in Mumbai, they landed in Bangalore. They checked into a hotel of their own choice, ditching the arrangements made by the concert organizers.

Room number 1002 was a luxury suite with a stunning view outside and cozy and clean inside.

'Do you have such good hotels in Pakistan?'

'Yes, we do, though I haven't got many chances to stay in such hotels in Pakistan until recently,' said Zoya beaming from ear to ear after inspecting the splendid bathroom.

Kabeer scratched his chin thoughtfully, 'If we remove the hatred that Indians and Pakistanis have for each other, you'll always find Pakistan and I'll always find India better. My point is, we strive to show our hospitality to each other's people more than our own, because we want them to think that we are better. And probably that's why I would never receive the kind of warmth I get here, in Pakistan.'

'We're in the right place then and I can feel less homesick,' Zoya smiled into his eyes, 'because there's only one person whom I love more than any country, and that is you.'

Kabeer could see the glow of her sculpted body in the black sleeveless top as she switched off the lights one by one. She left one light on and slipped into bed beside him. As Zoya tied up her hair in a ponytail, Kabeer caught a glimpse of her hairless and perfectly smooth underarms, which turned him on. She was too hard to resist at that moment.

'This night is going to be full of memories and I don't want you to forget the face of the person who made it memorable for you,' she said in a soft, silky voice.

'That's something,' Kabeer murmured as he cupped her face and kissed her luscious lips with increasing fervency until they tore off their clothes violently in a frenzy of passion. Zoya expected Kabeer to kiss her lips again but he lowered his mouth to kiss her other beauty. Zoya dug her nails into his back and clutched at his silky hair. She had never been loved like this before. Kabeer's tongue continued circling enticingly until Zoya, unable to control herself any longer, let herself go in orgasmic surrender as their bodies and souls became one. Kabeer and Zoya's lovemaking lasted late into the wee hours.

After they were fully sated with their love, they went to a bar called Toit Brewpub for a drink and then decided to take a romantic late-night stroll to enjoy what was left of the night.

They were in the elevator heading to their suite when Zoya received an upsetting message that her Bangalore concert had been called off. Apparently Pakistani militants had breached the border and had wounded an Indian soldier a few hours ago. Zoya put her phone away and ruminated crossly upon the ease with which Indians linked terrorism with Pakistan.

As per the organizer's instructions for the next event, Kabeer and Zoya were now scheduled to fly to Delhi on the next available flight the following day.

CHAPTER 37

October '16

In Delhi, Zoya was taken aside and thoroughly checked at the airport by security officials. Kabeer remembered that it had been just as difficult for him to clear security at Allama Iqbal International Airport in Lahore. Kabeer waited for almost an hour for Zoya to get through the procedures.

Zoya's eyes were heavy when she emerged and she pushed him away crossly when he comfortingly put his arm around her. Kabeer decided to give her some space.

'Thanks for not saying a single word to the policewomen who kept rechecking my stuff because of my nationality.'

'It would only have made the situation worse.'

'I stood up for you when you were on the verge of getting arrested, why didn't you do the same for me?' she asked bitterly when their car was speeding out of the airport.

'Your father is a powerful politician and you were able to pull strings. I don't have as much influence as you have, Zoya.'

'I wasn't on talking terms with my father, remember?' Zoya said. 'Also, you didn't stand up for me when that flat owner spoke ill of my country. Would that have diminished you as a patriot?'

'Zoya, do you honestly expect me to defy the security system of my nation when Indian soldiers were wounded less than a day ago. Do you want to see me behind bars? I too had a similar experience in Pakistan, but I didn't raise a hue and cry about it.'

'The problem is, I have come here to settle down with you, Kabeer. The least I can expect is for you to meet me halfway,' Zoya snapped.

'Sweetheart, I will cross the oceans to be with you. I know that it's tough for you now, but just give it a little more time and India will fall in love with you. We should realize that for our countries, each of us are outsiders. But every time someone points a finger at you, I can't help but think that I'm partly at fault too. Should I regret writing that letter? And what if you hadn't called me back that day? But when I see you sitting next to me, all my doubts vanish and my faith in our togetherness grows even stronger,' Kabeer hugged her. Zoya sighed and melted in his arms.

When they arrived at Taj hotel, they asked for the room that they had booked while they were still in Bangalore—701. 'Sorry sir, but you're two days ahead of schedule. However, we can offer you a room on the same floor, 702. Would that be all right?' asked the receptionist with a plastic smile on her face.

'Thanks,' replied Kabeer. They fell asleep holding each other, without making love, unaware of the storm bearing down on them. It would lead them down a road where they would come face to face with a reality that would change their lives forever.

CHAPTER 38

October '16

Three days later, Zoya delivered what was the most spectacular show of her life. Despite the unrest about the encounter at the border, the audience chanted her name so fervently that she wondered at herself for ever doubting the love of the Indians.

After the show, she received a lot of cards, sketches and Indo–Pak peace messages made by her fans, but what caught her eye was a beautiful portrait of her grandfather, Amaan Ali, and herself made by an old woman who seemed to be in her late eighties.

'I was one of the first ever Indian fans of Amaan sahib and I have sent my sketches and paintings to him regularly while he was alive. My name is Haseena Begum.'

Zoya remembered the lovely paintings in her house that her grandfather loved and the beautiful signature on each of them.

'Thank you so much, Dadi jaan,' Zoya hugged her. She exchanged numbers with her and Haseena gestured to her grandson to note down Zoya's number. The young man looked just as smitten with Zoya as his gran was with Amaan Ali. They vowed to keep in touch.

'India isn't that bad, Zoya,' Kabeer smiled to see her opinion of the Indians undergoing a change.

'It's the best,' she replied as she hugged him. 'Tonight was full of surprises. But there's yet another surprise that I want to give India tonight.'

'And what's that?'

'It wouldn't be a surprise if I told you,' Zoya said, her eyes bright with excitement. 'Anyway, you'll know very soon.'

People were filing out of the auditorium when Zoya ran up to the mic, 'I've got an important announcement to make.'

People stopped and turned around.

'A few months ago, I had my doubts about coming to India. I thought people would hate me for being a Pakistani, but let me tell you that my country, Pakistan, is as beautiful as India and the people there also yearn for peace just as you do. When I lost my grandfather while I was doing a concert in India, there was criticism from both countries, but there was one person who stood like a rock through all my good and bad moments and that's you, Kabeer,' she applauded and the people joined her, chanting 'Kabeer! Kabeer!' over and over again, until Kabeer was forced to step out of the wings and into the silver spotlight at Zoya's side.

'When I lost hope to live, you gave me breath,' Zoya continued smiling at him and clasped his hand in hers. 'When I was setting like a sun, you were there to tell me that I don't have to fear the night. You showed me that there's beauty even in the darkness as long as there's someone who truly loves me. I'm glad to have you in my life. Mere words cannot express how much I love you. Will you be mine forever, Kabeer?' Zoya smiled at Kabeer.

As Kabeer struggled with his emotions, a familiar voice came through the amplifier systems, 'First tell us, Zoya, which country is better? India or Pakistan?' Vishal Sharma stood by the footlights with a mic. 'Also,' he continued nastily, 'aren't you and Kabeer already sleeping together? The bottom line is, your land sponsors terrorism and killed those Indian soldiers. There's no denying you're a part of a terrorist state who's trying to make a name for yourself in India. There are also rumours rife about your grandfather being involved in terrorist activities—'

'Do not cross the line, Mr Sharma!' Zoya cut him off abruptly. 'Scandalmongers like you go beyond any limits for a scoop. My country is and always will be great; your country has also exported terrorism into Pakistan. Did you forget that?' Zoya choked on these words and added with a voice thick with unshed tears, 'Yours is a failed nation that has no qualms about thinking ill of its neighbours.'

Kabeer shook his head, wanting to comfort Zoya and at the same time disapproving of her rant.

'Wow! And what have we here,' scoffed Sharma, 'an Indian cricketer standing by as a Pakistani in India denounces his country,' Sharma hooted with raucous laughter.

The audience began to boo Zoya.

'Do you regret the killings done by the Pakistan army in India?' Sharma charged.

Zoya was on a roll now, nothing and nobody could stop her, not even Kabeer, 'I don't regret the killings done by the Pakistani army in India because you don't regret the killings done by the Indian army in Pakistan,' Zoya snapped, ignoring the fury in Kabeer's eyes.

A hush fell upon the auditorium as Kabeer finally spoke, 'Our worlds are different, Zoya. Our countries are different. Mine is a nation that seeks peace and yours, I am sorry to say, exports terrorism to the world at large. I was wrong to have assumed that a Pakistani would see and speak sense, but you're just as ignorant and violent as any other Pakistani.'

Zoya slapped him.

Silence.

Tears blurred Zoya's vision and her bosom heaved, 'This nonsensical person did her utmost to ward off all dangers and keep you safe in Pakistan.'

Her security personnel escorted her to the hotel before the storm finally arrived. Kabeer and Zoya broke their promise of undying love. She left India on the next flight, leaving the fragments of her broken heart behind.

Sometimes, life can change in the blink of an eye, leaving behind a lost hope that can never be rekindled. Sometimes, you have an answer to the questions life throws at you, but sometimes you get trapped by them, so much so that it's difficult for you to come out of them. Ever.

CHAPTER 39

April '17

Kabeer and Zoya went from being the international icons of love to a joke.

As much as a bad breakup takes from one, it also gives. It demonstrates the worth of each person in our lives. Sometimes the lessons learned after a breakup aren't the ones we expect.

Six months had passed and although Kabeer tried calling Zoya several times, she never answered or returned his calls. According to the media, she was dating a Pakistani popstar, Zaid, with whom she had been spotted on countless occasions. Zoya remained on Kabeer's mind despite all his efforts to forget her, and the gossip about her latest fling cut him to the quick.

Following a six-month sabbatical from cricket, Kabeer was determined to make his mark on the pitch again. Unfortunately, one day before the match, he got into a fracas with a reporter and was disqualified from the game.

Sometimes, the worst of your days can become the best and the discovery of the boarding pass to Bangalore felt just that to Kabeer.

The letter that he found at the end of the trail of clues indicated that he should journey to Pakistan, and the message in his own handwriting: 'I can't wait to see you now.' He felt giddy with all kinds of thoughts colliding and jostling in his head, and couldn't decide what to do. Ignoring the message would only underscore the finality of his goodbye to Zoya, a thought that filled him with agony. He couldn't imagine having to say those words to her nor could he imagine going through the same emotions again and again.

Kabeer kept wondering about the identity of the person who was leaving this trail of breadcrumbs for him. Why couldn't Zoya just call if she wanted to talk and get back with him? And if it wasn't Zoya but some sinister shadowy person, would it even be safe for him to go to Pakistan?

His phone rang at that moment. He was both surprised and alarmed to see that it was his grandfather calling. The old man didn't generally call him, unless it was urgent.

'I am in no mood to listen to your lies,' his grandfather started speaking before Kabeer could even greet him. 'Now tell me, where are you?'

'Delhi.'

'What are you doing there?'

'Someone, supposedly Zoya, left me a series of clues that led me here. I have travelled to Mumbai and Bangalore as well. And now the next clue is asking me to go to Pakistan.'

'What sort of clues are they?'

'Her boarding passes and a part of my handwritten letter.'

'Do you believe them?'

'I am not sure.'

'Just ask yourself.'

'I want to believe them.'

'Does that mean you want to go to Pakistan?'

'Yes.'

'Pack your bags. I'm coming with you.'

'It's not easy to get a Pakistani visa for an Indian.'

'I think it's high time I told you something that I've been keeping to myself for years. Plus, we'll leave in a week. I'll get a visa, you don't worry about that.'

His grandfather abruptly ended the call, leaving Kabeer with a multitude of questions swarming in his head. He desperately wanted to meet Zoya one last time.

He was about to make the most impulsive decision of his life and he wasn't sure where it would lead him but he swore to try and piece back together the fragments of his and Zoya's life one last time.

Against all odds, within ten days Kabeer and his grandfather set off on their journey to Pakistan.

CHAPTER 40

June 1947

Two friends sat in a lawn in the backyard of the two-storeyed house. A Hindu family lived on one floor and a Muslim family lived on the other.

'Why are you going to the other side of India?' asked Amaan.

'It's called the "Partition" and we have to live with our own people,' replied Yashwant sadly.

'But your people are here. Your friends are here, and I am here, Yashwant.'

'Naming a certain part of the land as India or Pakistan doesn't change anything—it's a place where we haven't ever lived,' Amaan protested. 'How does it matter what they call this land?'

'It would matter, Amaan. You're Muslim and I'm Hindu. We have to live on opposite sides of the border.'

'Have you already decided to leave Lahore?' Amaan scowled. 'You've already started saying "my people, your people".'

'That's how they're talking everywhere.'

'What matters is what we want. This is our house, Yashwant, and it will remain our house. It doesn't matter whether it lies in Pakistan or in India. Your people make your home and not vice versa.'

'You're Muslim and I'm Hindu, don't you understand? It's two different worlds now.'

'But neither of us is religious, anyway. I love celebrating Diwali and you love celebrating Eid with us. So what does religion have to do with where we live?'

'A nationality will be imposed upon you from August. We have been proud Indians until now and moving a few miles away from here won't change anything. There are Muslim people still living in India.'

'And I've seen Hindus choosing to remain here,' Amaan replied.

'You're putting words into my mouth as usual, Amaan.'

'I could say the same about you, Yashwant.'

'Time to go,' Yashwant's mother was carrying his younger brother on her hip and a suitcase in the other hand. His father was doing the heavy lifting, with a hold-all slung over his shoulder and a large suitcase in each hand.

The adults were trying hard to hold back their tears. It was a wrench to leave behind the people who were as good as family. They would now be a part of a different nation now. Yashwant wouldn't be able to play with Amaan any more or even see him. Nobody said anything because whatever had to be said was spoken through tears.

'Take some money. You'll have to build a new house there. But remember, you always have a home here in Pakistan.'

'You also remember that there's a home for you in India. You've paid for it already.'

Yashwant and Amaan stood by as their parents exchanged empty promises they knew they wouldn't be able to keep. It seemed highly unlikely that they would ever see each other again.

A bullock cart led away the sad procession. The two little boys were still mad at each other and didn't bother even waving goodbye.

Kabeer drifted into a trance-like state as he listened to his grandfather's story. He wanted to meet Zoya now more than ever. In his heart he knew they were meant to be together.

Yashwant was overjoyed to see his childhood home. He had left the place almost seventy years ago and had never expected to see it again.

CHAPTER 41

April '17

It had been a little more than sixty-nine years since Yashwant last stood in front of this house. Nothing much had changed apart from the wider roads and a few new constructions. He was surprised to see that his house had remained intact.

The house had been named after Zoya and Kabeer's great-grandmothers. Kabeer wondered why and how he hadn't noticed this before.

Kabeer rang the doorbell. There was no answer. He tried telephoning Zoya, but his cell phone wouldn't connect. His grandfather walked into the garden, gazing around with interest at the tall trees and beautifully manicured lawns. Kabeer waited for Zoya to answer the door.

After about half an hour, a car drove through the wide, wrought-iron gates and drove up to the portico. Zoya, more beautiful than ever, appeared both shocked and surprised to see him. Kabeer realized how much he had missed her over the past few months. He promised himself that he would never let her go again.

It was the moment Kabeer had been waiting for. He waited for Zoya to draw closer. She walked past, completely ignoring him. She left the door ajar, however.

He had run through this scenario so often in his head that he had convinced himself that he'd breeze through it and win her over in a matter of minutes. However, as he stepped inside, he found he was tongue-tied and his legs felt like jelly.

'Why are you here?' Zoya asked acidly.

Kabeer was nonplussed and wondered about the trail of boarding passes that had led him here. She seemed to have no clue about his strange adventure.

'I am here to finish the journey that we started together.'

'I too wanted that, but now I doubt if it can ever be possible,' Zoya replied, raising her eyebrows at Kabeer's grandfather seated on the steps of the porch. 'What is he doing here?'

'It's his house; he doesn't need permission to be here.'

'What the hell are you talking about?' Zoya scowled. Kabeer noticed a picture on the wall of two little boys sitting side by side. He had seen it before but hadn't attached any importance to it because at the time he hadn't known the story behind it. 'That picture, do you see it? That's your grandfather, with his arm around my grandfather. Their families lived together in this house before my grandfather was compelled to leave for India after Partition.'

Zoya looked at Kabeer's grandfather in amazement. She remembered her Naanu jaan talking about his childhood friend, Yashwant, who had moved to India in June 1947 and how he had desperately wanted to contact him. Zoya was overwhelmed with joy as she realized that, in a way, she had fulfilled her grandfather's wish of getting Yashwant back into this house where they had spent their childhood.

She started crying and hugged Kabeer.

'Thank you for coming back, Kabeer. I knew that you would return.'

'Then why all the drama? Why didn't you answer my calls and leave those random clues in the hotels? And when did you visit India?'

'I kept a very low profile on my last India trip and I was really happy that the media didn't get a chance to find me. We always talked about the randomness of our relationship and were proud of that and suddenly that night, that journalist broke us up in front of the world where we wanted to be the love story people got inspired by,' she replied. 'Everything ended that day but deep within I knew that you'd be going through the same pain as I was.'

'But why the boarding passes? What if I hadn't found them?'

'I wanted the universe to tell me if we deserved to be together or not. I wanted you to follow me to the ends of the earth and, most importantly, I wanted you to be sure of us getting back together,' Zoya smiled. 'You're special to me, Kabeer. I wanted to give us another chance.'

'Why? I didn't support you when you were in my country, proposing to me in front of the whole world. You were ready to be an Indian and I insulted you instead.'

'Yes and I slapped you. I have forgiven you for what you did, and I hope you can forgive me too. You did stand up for me in the strangest of ways, Kabeer. You've been my biggest and constant support from the time I met you. You have risked your life and based on a hint of a possibility, you followed me into the nation in which you were once attacked.'

'Haters don't belong to any specific nation. They're everywhere. But the Pakistanis have always loved me and the Indians have always loved you, Zoya,' said Kabeer. 'We're horribly flawed people, Zoya, and love is all about loving the best and accepting the worst. We are what we are and we'll be what we allow ourselves to be. We need to trust each other. Do you believe we could be the same people we once were?' Kabeer asked and Zoya embraced him and laid her head on his chest.

'We'll be better than that.' After a pause, she raised her head, 'So, what happens now?'

Kabeer laughed. 'Firstly, we'll have a romantic dinner tonight, make up for all the time we lost and promise to love each other forever. Be it Pakistan or India, we'll always be together, but we'll make our own world far away from all this hatred. I'll be your Pakistan when you need me to be and you'll be my India when I need you. We'll not be a different world for each other but be the best world for each other. This time, forever. I love you and I can't live without you.' Kabeer kissed her forehead. Yashwant was sitting in the bright sunshine on the patio watching his younger self playing with Amaan in the backyard. He chuckled deeply as the memories flashed by. It felt like yesterday to him.

'I'm back, Amaan,' he murmured, 'and I feel you're still here.'

My friend stepped on to the grass where we once played together and I felt alive again. He came into the backyard and there we were, frolicking together. He sat down on the porch where we had often sat together maligning our schoolteachers. I felt he touched my soul and embraced me.

Humans are a strange species, carrying their petty grudges forever and missing out on so much of love.

Now that I have met my dear friend again, I am at peace and can finally bid a happy goodbye to this world.

ACKNOWLEDGEMENTS

Love Knows No LoC, just like my other novels, couldn't have been written without the support of some people and it's important that I acknowledge all of them.

It's always difficult to acknowledge people, and a lot has changed in a year, but I am glad that there are certain relationships and people that haven't changed a bit.

Like always, I will begin by thanking my grandfather, Sohan Lal Vageria, for his unconditional love and blessings; my granny, Vibhuti Bandi, for always being so caring and cute. My parents, Dilip Vageria and Vandana Vageria, for being the loveliest couple ever and for their faith, undying support and encouragement. My elder brother, Ankit Vageria, for consistently believing in me and helping me with everything. You're the mastermind I always wished to be. Most importantly, for being the most important part of this story. This book would have been impossible without you, brother! My sister-in-law, Donika Vageria, for her unwavering faith in me; and to the world's cutest kid ever, my niece, Maahi Vageria, for still believing that her Chachu is a superman and can bring stars for her whenever she needs them. She has only grown cuter in the last one year. I can go on and on about her; she'll be more than proud to read this when she grows up as a beautiful young woman some day.

No thank you is enough for Swapnil Kothari sir, for being with me through every phase of my life and guiding me on what's right and wrong, both personally and professionally.

Some of the names without whom I consider my life incomplete and bland are: Aditi Solanki, for being the first person ever to praise my writing and making me believe that I can write and that people will read my books; Piyush, Rohit, Saloni, Novoneel and Romil, for being my best ever buddies and being there for me in the ups and downs of life and supporting me in the best possible way.

I am amazingly fortunate to have some lovely people in my life—Manoj, Abhishek, Saurabh, Pradeep, Himanshu, Shikha, Namita, Vinay, Pramod,

Pratik, Ulhas, Vankush, Ujjwal and Deep—who make my world better and more interesting.

Heartfelt thanks to some special people who have been fun company always: Saurabh sir, Naveen, Susmita, Sharanya, Sumit, Smita, Kunal, Meenu and Karan.

I would now like to thank my publisher for their extraordinary kindness and belief in my work. Thanks for being so supportive, Penguin Random House India, especially my editors, Gurveen and Indrani, who worked equally hard on this book.

I would like to thank Arup Bose, Jayant da and Stuti for working with me on three beautiful books.

Thanks to all my readers for believing in me. I love all your comments, reviews, emails and messages and I try my best to reply to each one of you. Thanks for making me work hard. Y'all have a big hand in making me what I am today. Keep giving me love and I shall keep writing many more stories.

And the most special thank you to the cutest girl who's my forever love, Pooja. More than anything else, she keeps me close to my dreams.

And lastly, to myself, for being able to complete this wonderful new book, *Love Knows No LoC*.